RejectGuy99

Richard A. Powell II

ISBN: 0692427686
ISBN-13: 978-0692427682

DEDICATION

For all you kids out there wondering what you could have done to deserve to being bullied, harassed, mistreated … NOTHING! All human beings should be respected and loved. Bullying is almost always about the bully and something they lack or are dealing with. The target is nothing more than a means to an end. In the moment, it's impossible to see that, and even later, often hard to accept. We do need thicker skins and many never learn how to build one. That would help, but never hinge your own happiness on how others treat you, and especially on how others view you. Vengeance won't help. Forgiving will not console. Living a full and happy life just being you, in spite of the past and the pain, is the only remedy.

ACKNOWLEDGMENTS

Thanks to Karen Boehle-Johnson and Darrel Messmore for reading this work early on and giving me invaluable feedback.

Thanks to author and editor extraordinaire Garrett Cook for helping me fine tune the book and discover its strengths and weaknesses. Your expertise is greatly appreciated.

I

CHAPTER ONE

My co-workers call me J-Dog but I don't really like the nickname. They don't know me that well, at least not outside of work, and since I've never spoken up on the issue, I guess I'll just have to deal with it. I'm just glad that anyone knows I exist at all because most of the time it doesn't feel that way. At ACME Computer Repair and Networking, I am treated with respect, mostly because I can diagnose and fix computer problems like Rain Man can do long division in his head. On the job, people come to me for help and they are grateful that I am part of the team, but that is where the admiration ends. Outside of work, I am a pariah, a nobody.

I'm just another videogame-playing, Mountain Dew-drinking, can't-get-laid nerd.

I love most of my work life. That's a positive. I hate most of my personal life. That's a negative. In algebraic terms, if you add a positive one and a negative one, you get me: a zero.

My actual name is Jackson. Jackson Reed, if you want to be more formal. I can't remember the last time someone called me by my real name. It's almost like I am two separate people with two completely different lives.

J-Dog spends forty-plus hours a week as a local computer demi-god. He reinstalls operating systems when people are careless with their web browsing, exposing them to viruses and such. He rescues their emails, their digital photos, their tax records, their genealogy research, and embarrassingly enough - their porn. He replaces bad hard drives and fried motherboards. The customers are desperate for help when they finally call ACME but are reluctant to pay a fair price for a geek to save their asses. J-Dog could be doing better but at least he feels important. He makes fifteen dollars an hour to keep people's virtual lives moving, cannot afford even subsidized medical insurance for all his trouble, and is so successful that he rides the bus to work because he can't afford a car.

Jackson, on the other hand, spends his time doing many things, most of them layered with thoughts about falling asleep and not waking up again, just so he can stop thinking about the gloom of his life.

He plays an insane amount of videogames, especially a particular one played online with other lonely and disenfranchised souls. He and his online friends gather in virtual space as mages and warriors and elves and orcs. They accept missions to rid villages of invading trolls or reckless bandits. They scour the world to build their skills and find hidden treasures. When a wyvern drops in on them, they run like hell. Their levels just aren't there yet, not for that kind of heat.

His screen name, RejectGuy99, is sad but true. He's a reject, he's a guy, and there is a 99 percent probability he always will be. The other players find his name funny and ironic. He finds the name depressing and a constant reminder of the state of his life. He's thought about changing it dozens of times - his screen name, not his life. Unfortunately, he's too much of a chicken-shit to do anything about his pitiful life, and since everyone already knows him by that screen name and creating a new one would just be one big pain in the ass - it stays.

So as you can see, my life is a series of highs and lows, but lately, the lows are winning out. Once I leave work, very few people even know I'm alive, and it's been that way for years. In all honesty, I'm not sure if I bring this on myself - my sheltered nature and reserved personality playing a cruel life trick on me - or if the Universe has just seen fit for my social existence to be scarce and hollow. Either way, the pain is the same.

The China Station and Big Louie's Pizzeria know me by name, and even at the sound of my voice they already know what I want. Nothing real there. I am perfectly predictable. Despite the familiarity within my favorite eateries, I still lack significant and real relationships with other human beings. The brief discussions with the employees of my favorite establishments about sweet and sour chicken and sausage, mushroom, and pepperoni thin crust pizza are nothing more than desperate attempts to prolong meaningless conversations, waiting for genuine connections to other human beings, anyone at all. Unfortunately, the bond never clicks. My life remains pathetic. Most days, I wish I hadn't woken up at all.

CHAPTER TWO

I really, really ... REALLY hate Mondays. In the world of PC support, especially with my company where there are no weekend hours, Mondays represent the equivalent of being dropped at the base of Mount Everest at 7 a.m. and being asked to reach the peak by noon. Over the average weekend, my company receives more than a hundred emails and several dozen phone messages from customers desperately needing help to fix some computer problem; twenty-five percent of which are user error, and roughly fifty percent that can be fixed with a simple reboot.

Computers are not perfect devices, not by a long shot. And sometimes, a tiny glitch can occur whereby nothing is truly wrong - the dang thing just needs to go back to bed and start the day over again. Reboot.

The sunlight pierces my burnt orange and gray jacket while I stand at the bus stop. It sends a shiver through my body as it warms me nicely. There is a slight chill in the fall air and it immediately makes me think of pumpkin pie. Great, now I'm hungry. I didn't have breakfast and only brought a Ham and Swiss sandwich for lunch. I guess I'll have to grab some mini-donuts from the vending machine when I get in. I can't really afford it, honestly, but knowing the shit-storm I'm about to fall into from the weekend backlog, I'm going to need brain food. Standing here fantasizing about food completely drowns out the almost deafening sound of traffic whizzing by, horns buzzing, construction and industry throbbing all around.

I snap from my trance as the bus labeled Green #5 pulls in front of me. The brakes squeal relentlessly as it comes to a stop in a screeching rendition of nails on a chalkboard. I shake my head as if I can remove the noise from my ears by tossing it around. The usual puff of hydraulics precedes the doors sliding open. I step up and in, wave and smile at the driver Charlie, punch my bus-pass, then take my seat directly behind him.

I don't like being anywhere except the front of the bus. It greatly decreases my chances of encountering a piss or puke puddle, and the beginning of the week is hard enough to endure without slipping in a hobo mess. As a veteran rider, I've picked up on many of these unwritten rules of riding the transit. That one is the most critical. We'll call it bus riding tip number one. I might share more later if I feel the need.

The bus drops me off right in front of ACME and I can see Carlos Villegas, my geek-in-training, waiting at the doors for me. I'm about five foot-nine, and I'd say he's about two inches shorter than I am, but he's extremely fit and athletic looking, quite the opposite of me with my ever growing pot belly. I'm not obese, by any means, but definitely overweight and under expansion. I really need to be careful and lay off the Dew. I hear they're calling pizza a vegetable now in schools, in which case, I'm not doing too bad. Joke.

I am the first person to get in, as I am the one assigned to begin the process of dealing with the weekend backlog. Most everyone else starts at 8:30 a.m. and works until 5, and though my starting time is fixed, I go until the work is done and am the only one allowed to actually work overtime. Being the resident PC guru, there is simply no one else that does what I do at the company, so there isn't much choice. Thankfully, they have hired Carlos for me to train. That way, I have a partner who can cover for me when needed, and perhaps lighten my workload and ultimately keep me from burning out, which would be disastrous for them.

This help I am receiving all came about from an incident that occurred about two months back.

After a particularly gruesome week of nationwide computer virus hell, I finally blew a gasket when I couldn't get a processor seated correctly on a motherboard. My hands had trembled as I worked that day, small rumblings of the coming earthquake. I did not heed the warning. In an uncharacteristic act of aggression and finally at my wits end, I stood up from my work table, grabbed the motherboard, and launched that sucker twenty feet across the room. The collision with one of the many metal racks that line the back wall of our workshop sent green plastic shards in all directions. I let out a spine-chilling, primal scream that more than startled everyone in the front of the store.

My boss, Henry Walsch - a tall, lanky character, who is extremely non-confrontational and way too touchy-feely and huggy-huggy, rushed back to the workshop. When he saw my face and the rage brewing, I was sure he was going to throw-up or something. He didn't, thank god, but I'm sure the incident tested every fiber of his being.

I screamed at him. "There is way too much fucking work to do for one person around here and I'm tired of it! You either hire someone to help me or I quit!"

Henry just stood there in shock. We had never once even had an argument, let alone me raise my voice and lash out physically. He got one word out, "Well..."

I cut him off. "I'm going home. If you want to fire me, fine. I'm taking the rest of the day off. You can leave me a message if you want me to come back tomorrow." In a rage, I went to the break room, snatched all my stuff, and stormed out to wait at the bus stop for the next available ride home. He didn't say another word and no one tried to stop me. Luckily, he called later that day and apologized for not hiring someone sooner, and told me that he already had someone in mind that might be a good fit. He then proceeded to schmooze me with compliments regarding my amazing talents and how wrong it was for them to take advantage of me. If anything good came out of that incident, other than getting Carlos to train, it was that I got a raise and an extra week's vacation for my trouble. Still not what I think I deserve, but fifteen dollars an hour is better than twelve, so I guess I won't complain too much. Maybe I can afford to get a used car now. How awesome would that be?

"Hey, Carlos. Have a good weekend?"

"It was okay. Didn't do much. Just hung around the house mostly. How 'bout you? Any hot dates?" Carlos flashes a couple of quick eyebrow lifts at me.

I can only assume he wants me to share the juicy details of my blossoming love-life. Correction – imaginary love-life. Is this guy smoking crack?

"Dude, seriously? I don't think I said two words to another human being over the weekend, at least not in person. I'm not exactly a ladies' man." I grab my slightly bulging belly and give it a good shake to demonstrate my lack of physical appeal. I'm about twenty-five pounds overweight now and I desperately need to lay off the soda and Hostess Ding Dongs, but they keep me sharp while gaming after a long day at work. Plus, they're cheap when I buy them at the warehouse store.

I unlock the metal-framed glass front door of the shop and we enter the building heading straight to the break room to drop off our stuff. I flick all the light switches in the building on as we go. We each put our personal items into our assigned lockers and head to The Lab, our nickname for the workshop and the biggest room at ACME. It measures about thirty feet by thirty-five feet and all the outer walls are covered with freestanding metal racks, each one of those with five particle board shelves chock full of hard drives, motherboards, computer cases, laptop keyboards, and all other manner of PC fodder. There is also one filing cabinet by the entry door where I keep instruction manuals and the like. There are two baskets sitting on top where the work orders are placed, one incoming, one outgoing. The inner part of the room has four large banquet-style tables, each twelve feet long with various rolling desk chairs surrounding them. Those tables and chairs are where I spend most of time, as does Carlos.

For a Monday, we actually have a relatively quiet start to the day. Having someone to train and work with also makes the time go faster. I sure hope he works out, and more importantly, stays. After just six weeks, he has quickly picked up the routine, and though he doesn't have the knowledge and experience I do, he is fast approaching a skill level that will soon rival my own. I couldn't be happier. I guess I should throw a motherboard against the wall more often around here. Maybe they'll make me part owner. I can dream.

I keep a phone at the main table I work at, as well as a laptop, so I send Carlos to boot up all the front-line computers and printers while I start listening to the messages left over the weekend. Sweet relief. There are only two messages, both asking for the status of computer repairs that are already being worked on. I cannot recall a time when we had so few phone messages from the weekend.

My laptop finishes loading, so I bring up Outlook to go through the emails. Thirty new ones in the inbox - that's not too bad. I quickly scan through each one, moving them into different folders based on their needs. Only one goes into the URGENT folder. That's another surprise. If things keep going this smoothly, this will be the best Monday ever. I cross fingers on both hands and ask god for continued calm.

Carlos returns and sits on the other side of the table and boots up his work laptop. We spend the next hour and a half filling in the weekly spreadsheet where we keep track of all the ongoing projects. Each job is assigned a number, at this time six digits with a letter at the end that represents the first letter of the customer's last name. We type in a brief description of the problem and the work that will be performed, then we put a start date and estimated finish date for the job. This information is accessible by the front-line staff so they can communicate with the customer at any time without bothering us.

By the time Henry and Meghan show up, I am ready for a fifteen minute break but I am no longer hungry, so I just sit in the break room alone, pondering the emotions I had dealt with over the weekend. I struggle sometimes with understanding my purpose in life. I often wonder what the road ahead of me will hold because when I try hard to look, all I see is a blur with flashes of a stagnant, ordinary, lonely existence. If only my home life could rival my work life, even a little, then maybe I wouldn't feel like such a loser sometimes. How can I live such an ambivalent existence? I want nothing more than both sides of me to unite into a meaningful and powerful person, not this two-headed, half-genius, half-idiot mess that I am today. Something really needs to change. I'm growing tired of the battle.

I spend the rest of the morning coasting through my assigned jobs and barely speaking, my negative mood lingering like a diseased aura around my body and my mind. Carlos and I are at different tables, seating and reseating processors, video cards, and RAM memory. We place jumpers over small metal prongs, tightening and loosening a thousand tiny little screws that are impossible to locate once they hit the floor.

At lunch, Carlos and I sit in the break room but neither of us says a word. I take two bites of my sandwich but start to feel sick, so I throw it away. Spoiled deli meat? Maybe, then again, I barely ate anything over the weekend, just a half a box of dry Lucky Charms, and if you can believe it, very little soda. I actually drank water for once in my life. Overall, I think I've lost my thirst and appetite. I can only assume I have some kind of stomach bug, but I won't be seeing a doctor. No insurance. I guess I'll just have to tough it out.

The afternoon work is uneventful and I am able to leave around 4 p.m. From my usual seat on the bus, I stare at the passing traffic and buildings as we go. Stop to stop, people come and go. I'm so lost in thought I almost miss my own stop. The doors open and everyone is still. Luckily, the driver and I are friendly and familiar, so he shouts to rouse me from my trance.

"Jackson! This is you!"

I shake my head and return to the world of the living, grab my bag and lunch box, and hurry down the steps, saying thanks with a wave as I hit the sidewalk. I need something to help me alter my attitude and I know exactly what will do the trick: game night.

CHAPTER THREE

Our usual weekday game nights generally start at six and end around nine. We have a great team. All of us even live around here, but oddly enough, I've never met any of them. I don't even know their real names. There have been discussions about doing a LAN party, though my reticent nature holds me back. I admit it would be fascinating to get together and finally meet. Of course, they're all on social media together and I'm the lone holdout on that front. I've created images in my mind, however, as to their appearances. How closely would my imagination mirror reality? I doubt they'd be too impressed with me.

After showering, I heat a frozen dinner in hopes I will be able to pick away at it mindlessly as I play. I'm still not feeling a hundred percent, so I situate myself in bed with my laptop and make my way into the world of online gaming. I won't bore anyone with the details of the game we play, suffice it to say, it's a major one. There are many people who have lost years of their lives playing this game to excess. My team is dedicated and we play often, but none of us will lose sleep or our jobs or our families because of the obsession. It's a perfectly healthy outlet for people who don't enjoy the outdoors, and for those of us who have nothing better to do anyway.

Online Conversation before starting the game –

RejectGuy99:   Hey team. Waz the happy-haps?
2NE1-KPopper: Asian Flava in da house
1LonelyGurl: Hey fellas. Ready 2 go here
ScoobyDont69:   Good   here.   How   was everyone's weekend?

1LonelyGurl: Work is crazy busy right now. I could get called in soon, so it might be a short night for me

:-(

RejectGuy99: That sucks LG. I soooo need this game 2nite

2NE1-KPopper: My parents made me visit my Grammie at the nursing home. I NO LIKE!

ScoobyDont69: Manic Monday RG? & KPop, no like Grammie or nursing home? And if u moved out of ur parents basement - FREEDOM! *braveheart-just watched it

1LonelyGurl: Why don't u cum over here RG and I'll make it all better for u

;-)

2NE1-KPopper: My grams is OK. Nursing home smell funny. Bleh

RejectGuy99: Ehhh. Just a lil depressed. Stupid really. And LG, don't tease, I might just show up at ur door

1LonelyGurl: Anytime ur man enough RG

;-)

ScoobyDont69: Whoa! Get a room u 2. Seriously, u guys need to just do it and get it over with. ☺ I feel like the 4 of us are trying to ride a 2-seater tandem bike. Awkward!

ScoobyDont69: Ya know, RG, maybe it's time for u to break out and expose yourself 2 us. We're all friends on Facebook, yet u remain hidden away. What do ya say?

2NE1-KPopper: YES! Life 2 short

RejectGuy99: Tempting. But u guys know how I feel about social networking. No privacy. I might get the balls one of these days to meet in person. Maybe ... soon

2NE1-KPopper: Yo homies, can we please get playin'. I need to slay some MFers! And probably bag a ho. That's juss me, it's what I do

1LonelyGurl: Yes, let's play. KPop - the manwhore - needs some virtual be-boppin. And no pressure RG

ScoobyDont69: Sounds good. Let's do it! Game on!

RejectGuy99: Alllllllll-righty then. Meet at the Tavern

An hour later–

1LonelyGurl: Sorry guys, just got the call ;-(

RejectGuy99: Noooooooooo!!! That sucks

2NE1-KPopper: Me no like. Have fun at work

ScoobyDont69: I gotta work early 2morrow anyway

RejectGuy99: *sigh*

1LonelyGurl: I'll be free Fri 4 sure, full game night. I'll make it up to u guys. Be good

2NE1-KPopper: Laterz. Peace Out!

ScoobyDont69: Have a good rest of the week all. Same time Friday

RejectGuy99: Catch u all Fri then

1LonelyGurl: BBL – OTSAL

That was a little disappointing. I was so looking forward to a long, successful gaming campaign with my online friends tonight. I can't blame LG. She is a nurse and gets called in occasionally when staff is short. Her sign-off, BBL – OTSAL says it all: Be Back Later – Off To Save A Life. That's way more important than any stupid game. It's just that the only time in my personal life I don't feel so isolated is when gaming. I only wish I had the balls to act on the playful banter between LG and me. I'm not sure if she is just being nice or what, but then again, she doesn't say those suggestive things to the other guys on the team, only me.

I did notice while playing and chatting that I could barely feel my growing stomachache, though I hardly touched my dinner. I kept pecking away at it between keystrokes, but ultimately, I ate only about a quarter of it. Even my 32-ounce plastic cup of Mountain Dew sat neglected, now watered down by the ice, condensation resting along the sides and soaking the twice-folded paper towel I placed beneath it.

Apparently, my thirst and appetite have disappeared. I'm not sure if I should be worried or not. My physical symptoms are minor. Maybe it's just the stress, though work has been much less so lately, especially with Carlos working out so well. I've put in just over forty hours each of the last three weeks, which is a far cry from the usual fifty or sometimes even sixty that I have come to expect. I've just been so depressed and broken the past month.

My life is not always so bad. There are fleeting moments when I smile wide, feel content, but...

When the laptop screen goes dark at night and I am lying in bed alone with only my thoughts to occupy me, I get lost in emptiness. Even in my own imagination, in the corners of my mind that no one will ever know but me, I am weak and scared, still that nine-year-old boy who suffered and cried while enduring horrible things. Even now, as a grown man, I cannot shake that version of myself from atop my shoulders, as it clings too tight to ever let go. I want it to. Oh, how I want it to.

If I'm going to be honest with myself, I suppose I do know the real reason I've been in this state lately. A month ago, while shopping at my local warehouse store, I ran into my foster parents, the ones who took me in after my real parents died when I was just nine years old. I have no other family and thus became a ward of the state. After only a few months at The Banner Smith Children's Home, I joined the foster care system. I had already been coping with a child's worst nightmare, but then it seemed like I had been thrown into a barrel of gasoline, set on fire, and rolled off a cliff. I'm sure there are great foster parents out there that nurture and properly care for their foster kids, but my personal experience is with only one family, and they did not care about helping me. They were, in a word, evil. I was subjected to mental, emotional, and physical abuse by both foster parents and their two sons, both of whom were older than me. They did their fair share of bullying and torturing - enough that I've come to view them in the same light as their parents.

One thing is for certain - no one will ever hear me use their names. I, one hundred percent, refuse to call them by their real names. They are nothing more than Foster Father, Foster Mother, Foster Brother number one, and Foster Brother number two. These are the legal definitions of their relationship to me on paper. I find their actual natures to be inhuman, so they get no more respect from me than that.

So while shopping on a Saturday afternoon, there they were. I had not seen or spoken to them since the day I turned eighteen and moved out of their house. That was easily the best day of my life. I was free from their torment - at least in body - but my spirit remains a prisoner. I can't believe I'm still letting them affect my life. How does one forget about nine years spent in hell? I equate it to trying to forget that I have brown hair and brown eyes or that I'm a little overweight and always have been. All these things are a part of me that cannot be denied. I guess I could dye my hair, get colored contacts, go on a diet, but that change would only be on the surface, and just like my past, the truth of who I really am will always remain inside. My brown eyes will still be hiding under the contact lenses. The roots of my brown hair will soon emerge from the cheap dye job; all of them still lingering inside - just like my past.

I get out of bed and take my dinner and cup into the kitchen. After thinking about it for a few seconds, I toss the food in the trash and dump the watered-down soda in the sink. It dawns on me that I can't remember the last time I peed. I know I haven't been eating or drinking much, but with as much soda as I drink, I typically go to the bathroom often. That's another thing to put on my list of body and behavioral oddities for the week.

I head back to the bedroom and decide to just catch up on a few shows to help clear off some of the DVR. While I sit in the dark watching television for three hours, my stomach starts to hurt again and now a slight pain in my back pops up, on the right hand side. I let out a huge sigh.

"Jesus, I'm falling apart here."

If I intend to sleep, I figure I better take something for the pain, so I lean over and pull open the top drawer of my nightstand. Sitting just inside and on top of everything else is a flyer I yanked off a telephone pole while waiting for the bus a few weeks ago. I'm not sure why I grabbed it to begin with, but for some reason it called to me.

I pull it out and read - *Feeling depressed, lonely, sad, helpless? There is hope. You are not alone. Life is worth living. Just call and tell us how you're feeling.*

We can help. 1-877-555-2424. Crisis Intervention Hotline. Safe. Confidential. Here when you need us.

They really hit the nail on the head with that flyer. Pretty much sums it up for me right now. I think about tossing it in the trash, but instead I just place it face down on the top of my nightstand and snatch the ibuprofen. I take the bottle into the bathroom and open it up, shake out two pills and pop them in my mouth, using my hand to cup some water to wash them down.

I stare at the chubby fucker looking back at me in the mirror. "What an ugly loser. LG would be mortified if she ever met you. She seems way too cool and has a great career and everything going for her. What could she possibly ever see in a train-wreck like you? Nothing, that's what. She represents nothing more than just another thing in your life that will always remain at a distance. A tease and a constant reminder of how pitiful you are and how pointless your life is. Idiot. Worthless. Moron. Stupid."

Time for bed, I don't want to think about my life anymore. Lights out.

CHAPTER FOUR

"Oh god! I can't throw up anymore. Uhhh. What in the hell is wrong with me?"

I take a few deep breaths, slow and deliberate, trying with every last bit of willpower not to vomit again. It's been off and on for the last thirty minutes. I've hardly eaten anything in two days, so at first the food came up, but now it's mostly dry heaves and a little bile. That can't be healthy. I'm going to have to break down and see a doctor if this doesn't let up soon.

When the upward movement ceases, I get ready for work and head out to the bus stop, triple-layered plastic bag in hand, just in case. I cut the timing a little too close for comfort but make it to the bench with a minute to spare.

That brings up bus riding tip number two: Arrive at the bus stop at least five minutes before the scheduled pickup time. My experience has shown that buses have a differential in arrival times of plus or minus three minutes, so if you show up five minutes early, you will never miss your ride. I've never once seen a bus show up more than five minutes early and never more than five minutes late. These are words to live by for all the riders out there who give a crap.

I sit for the entire ride to work with my eyes closed, one hand on my forehead. I look at my phone often to help me gauge when my stop is getting near.

Once the bus screeches to a halt, I exit gingerly and walk slowly to the door. Carlos is already here. On a day like today, I sure am glad he joined ACME. With my health and mind spiraling out of control, his presence will help alleviate any guilt I might carry if I need to take some time off.

"Damn, J-dog! You don't look too fuckin' good. You all pale and shit and your eyes are wicked bloodshot. You okay?"

I cover my eyes in embarrassment. I hadn't really noticed but the way I feel on the inside has manifested outward.

"I didn't sleep very well, plus I threw up a bunch this morning." I unlock the door and we enter. I slowly work my way to the break room while Carlos turns on all the front line equipment and the lights. I plant my butt in a chair and put my head down on the table with my eyes closed. Now that I'm here, I barely have the energy to move.

Carlos joins me at the table. "You need to see a doctor."

"Probably. I just really don't want to. Damn hassle is what it is."

"Tell you what man, just stay in here and rest until the boss comes in. I'll take care of all the morning crap." Carlos rises from the table and heads toward the workshop. "You want me to turn off this light?"

"Sure ... and thanks man. I owe you one." I keep my head down and my eyes closed, trying to ignore the pain radiating through my body. I feel a tightening on the right side of my lower back like a pulse in time with my heartbeat. I wince about every third one. This really sucks. Why did I even bother to come in today?

I'm startled awake by Carlos' tap on my shoulder. I wasn't even aware he had turned the light on or that I had been asleep for forty-five minutes.

"Hey man. Time to wake up. Henry'll be here in a few minutes. Better get your shit together and hit the workshop. I got us all set for the day."

"Thanks again, Carlos." My voice is frail. I swallow hard trying to coat my burning throat and quell the acid burn. I rub the sleep from my eyes and yawn long and wide. I get up from the table, put my jacket and bag in my locker, and slog into the workshop. My mind is sluggish, I don't even hear the bell of the front door until Henry is standing right next to me. I jump and turn to face him when I sense his presence.

"Oh jeez! You scared the crap outta me."

"Hey, J-Dog. You all right? You don't seem well," Henry says as he puts his hand on my shoulder.

"I haven't been feeling too good. Got sick before work today and really haven't felt right for a few days."

"Why on Earth did you come in today? You should have called me. Grab your stuff. I'll give you a lift to your apartment."

I just nod and walk back to my locker. There is no point in arguing. I don't think he would have taken no for an answer, and really, I'm kind of relieved at the prospect of being able to go back to bed.

"Carlos, you going to be okay here without J today?"

"Yeah boss. I got this covered. Not a lot going on today anyways."

"Good. I'll be back shortly. Keep an eye on the front line until Meghan gets in."

I join Henry and wave goodbye to Carlos.

"Get some rest man. And go to the damn doctor 'fore you drop dead."

I just nod in acknowledgement, no intention of following through.

Henry and I head out to his car, a black Toyota Camry with a tan interior, clean. Neither one of us says anything until we're about halfway to my apartment. I keep making little sounds when I feel the throbbing pain in my back.

"You sure you don't want me to take you to the hospital? You look really bad, Jackson."

That's weird. He called me Jackson.

"No. I'll be okay. I just need to rest. Plus, I can't really afford it."

"I'm not sure you can afford not to. Can't have you dropping dead now."

He is trying to keep the tone light but I can tell he is really concerned, and hell, so am I.

I have no idea what is wrong with me. I haven't gone to the bathroom in almost two days, my back is killing me, and I had the worst case of nausea and dry heaves I can ever remember having. It's not like this has been going on for a while now either, the whole thing just popped up suddenly, and it went from zero to sixty in four seconds.

We pull into the parking lot of my complex and I point him in the direction of my place. The lot is half empty with most people already gone for the day.

We both get out of the car and Henry walks me to my front door.

"I want you to call me before you come in tomorrow. If you're still not feeling well, take the day off and go see a doctor ... or I'm going to drag you to one."

He is surprisingly stern and father-like. He's usually much more timid. I can't tell if his feelings are genuine for me as J-Dog, the ACME employee, or for me as Jackson, fellow human being, and dare I say, friend.

I finally nod. "I'll talk to you first thing in the morning either way." I unlock my front door and swing it open, taking one step in.

"I can't have J-Dog, ACME's super-geek, missing in action for too long."

And there I have my answer.

"But ACME be damned. You need to take care of yourself because there are people who care about you, and not just because of what you mean to ACME."

And now I'm confused and getting a little choked up. "Thanks, Henry. That means a lot to me." There is an awkward pause.

"Well, get some rest and just call me tomorrow. You need anything right now?"

"I'm good. Thanks again. Talk to you in the morning." I place a little finality on the words to try and end the conversation. I wave goodbye. He waves back and nods as he turns to leave.

After shutting the door and locking it, I fall back against it and cry. Confusion eclipses my mind. I don't trust people. No surprise there. I have a hard time believing that Henry really gives a crap about me as a person. He sure seemed for real, but then again, Henry is the kind of guy who just oozes empathy. I'm just lucky he didn't try to hug me.

I stop crying, clutch my fists and shake them in the air, and let out a deep, five second scream of frustration. My face is undoubtedly red. The blood rushes to my head and gives me an instant headache. I bend down in pain, dropping my jacket and bag at the door. I stand straight up again, too tired to even think anymore. I walk to my bedroom, turn the box fan on high to drown out any middle of the day noises, strip off my shoes, shirt, and pants, and crawl under the covers, asleep in just a couple of minutes.

CHAPTER FIVE

I wake and there is no light creeping around the blinds in my bedroom. I've never slept this long before in my life, but I think it helped as I don't feel too bad. Actually, I think I need to go to the bathroom.

I hop out of bed and rush to the toilet. Suddenly, I need to pee urgently. I barely get the front of my underwear down in time for the stream. The initial relief is quickly followed by intense pain in my bladder. I look down and see my urine is discolored with a small amount of blood. Considering how urgent the feeling was to go, the stream ends prematurely and reduces to a trickle. When I'm done, I don't immediately flush, I just glare into the toilet, the hope that my health troubles were coming to an end fades fast.

This is just my luck. As I walk to the kitchen to get a drink, the pain in my back nearly floors me. I fall against the wall of the hallway, just short of the entrance to the kitchen. The pulsating ache spreads to my entire lower abdomen.

"Ahhh!" I stay leaning against the wall, hoping I don't end up on the ground. "I need something to take away this pain. It's getting ridiculous."

A spark of inspiration floods my head. I don't drink very often, so I have very little tolerance for hard liquor, but alcohol would sure do the trick right now. I think the last time I even had a beer was at the ACME Christmas dinner. I bet some whiskey would knock my ass right out. My stomach is still gurgling with acid too, so I think some Pepto-Bismol is in order. Luckily, there is a convenience store just around the corner from my apartment building.

I stand still and brace myself against the wall for five minutes before the pain becomes tolerable enough for me to get dressed: sweatpants, a hoodie, and some sandals are all I can manage without further discomfort. I make sure to grab my cell phone, just in case, and hunched over like Quasimodo, I gingerly walk, if you can call it that, to the Get-In/Get-Out around the corner.

I don't see another person on the sidewalk as I go but I can imagine women and children screaming and running in all directions as I approach.

My god, what the hell is it? Jimmy, walk faster, or better yet, let's cross the street real quick. Faster, boy. The thing will get you if you don't hurry.

What is it, mommy?

I don't know, Jimmy, but I imagine it's what happens to someone when they run from their emotional baggage and don't eat enough veggies.

Do I have emo baggage, mommy?

I'm working on it, baby.

Your results may vary but it's not far from truth.

The electronic bell sounds as I enter the right hand side of the double glass doors. I had a hell of time pushing the door open at first. I don't remember it being so damn heavy. Coming off the darkness from outside, the brightly lit store forces me to squint. I stand just inside the door for a few seconds to wait for my eyes to adjust.

There are maybe six other people in the store, not including the clerk. I turn to the left to hit the booze aisle when I catch a glimpse of my reflection in the doors. A leper. That's what I look like. I don't have sores or anything, obviously, but I'm hunched over, pale, and just sickly. My self-conscious nature takes over and I'm sure everyone in the store is now staring at me, which increases my stress levels ten-fold. I push through the pain and do my best to rush to the hard liquor section. I grab the first bottle that stands out, some J.D., then head to the medicine aisle.

I'm perusing the antacids when I glance over and see a section labeled Sleep-Aids. Should the alcohol not do the trick, a sleeping pill might help me get more rest. Other thoughts, dark thoughts, swirl in my mind too but I try not to entertain those voices.

I snatch the cheapest sleeping pills off the shelf, and for good measure, take a bottle of the pink stuff too. I don't want to seem like a complete loser at the checkout. I'm feeling judged already. My eyes dart to and fro, checking to see if the other patrons are watching me. I don't see anyone but I know they're around, lurking behind racks of salty snacks and pallets of soda and cheap beer.

I set the goods down on the counter and shove them toward the clerk.

"This all for ya?" Mallory asks. She's the weekday evening clerk who knows me by name but who I hope doesn't recognize me. I refuse to make eye contact.

"Yes," I answer briskly and with a slightly raspy voice. I'm not sure if I did it intentionally or not, but I cannot deny the likelihood it was an act to help in hiding my identity.

Mallory rings up each product after turning them one by one to see their tags. "That'll be thirty-eight dollars and thirty-two cents. You need a bag?"

I nod. The total startles me a bit. I didn't bother to check the prices on any of the items I picked up. I suppose the sticker shock is unjustified. What did I expect? I'm buying drugs and alcohol from a corner store. Duh.

She places the three items in a brown paper bag as I pull two twenty dollar bills from my wallet. There goes all my weekly spending money, not that I will need it for anything this week considering my illness, except perhaps an emergency room visit if I can't shake this soon.

I slide the bills across the counter and sneak a peek at Mallory. I catch her looking right at my face, probably trying to figure out my problem, and who I am. She hands me my change, which I hastily stuff into the front right pocket of my sweats, then I grab the bag around the throat of the bottle. Before I can pull away, surprise crosses her face.

"Jackson? I almost didn't recognize you. Are you okay?"

"I ... uh ... hi." Suddenly, my voice is back to normal. Stupid. "I'm fine, Mallory. Just not ... feeling well. See ya later." I don't even wait for her to respond. I bolt from the store, using all my strength to press the door open with my lowered shoulder, ignoring the excruciating pain in my abdomen and back.

Just before the door seals behind me, she says, "Take it easy."

I waste no time getting some liquid relief. Once I hit the edge of the property and a poorly lit area, I unscrew the bottle and take a huge swig. I gag from the fumes and the taste.

"Oh boy." I smack my lips repeatedly. "Aye Carumba!" My face flushes and I am instantly hot and sweating. I take another drink, half the size of the first one. The effect is no less intense. I shake my head, take a few deep breaths, and screw the cap back on the bottle. "I better get home before my legs give out on me. Or before I forget where I live. That would suck."

I get back to my apartment physically unscathed. The booze is already helping my pain, but my mind is turning and turning with bad thoughts. I cannot erase the image of my foster parents at the warehouse club. FM always had a way of slipping subtle little insults into any conversation when I was growing up, and the bitch just couldn't help herself when we met face to face a month ago.

Sheer horror crawled up my spine as our shopping carts approached. I'm sure my face told the story. I'm generally a nice person by nature, even with my difficult past, so I knew I would be cordial during the encounter. The question was: how would they react? I got my answer with the first words out of FM's mouth.

"Jackson," FF plainly acknowledged with a nod.

"I see you've moved up in the world," spat FM with a smirk on her face that said everything.

Granted, I had grubby shorts on and a dirty inside-out shirt, but it was laundry day and I was bumming it for the weekend, so I didn't exactly make a great impression. I don't think it would have mattered. She would have found something snotty to say regardless. I just found it disheartening and classless that the first words that came out of her mouth after so many years were criticism. It reminded me why I left.

I looked down at my outfit and shrugged. I immediately fell back into the role of foster child: timid, spineless, and full of excuses. "Laundry day. I didn't realize I would see anybody I knew." That was a Freudian slip if there ever was one. I once knew them but certainly I no longer wanted to know them.

We just stared at each other for a few moments but didn't say anything. I had nothing good to say, so I held my tongue, barely. In that moment, the entire nine years' worth of bullshit flooded my mind, and only the bad memories came forward - the worst of the worst. To this day, I still have a difficult time recalling some of the good things that occurred during my time with them.

I have to think long and hard to remember winning my class Spelling Bee in fifth grade, or to remember finishing second place in a computer programming competition against other high schools when I was in ninth grade. Those were shining moments in my childhood that I rarely think about. Both of those amazing incidents, of course, were paralleled with equally shitty encounters with the foster parents, especially her. She saw only failure in my actions, flukes, coincidence. My Spelling Bee win had apparently been possible because the smartest kid in class was out sick, and my programming achievement was negated by the fact that I didn't win. Second place is for losers, she said.

"Well, I gotta go. See ya," I said, breaking the awkward free-flowing nothingness. I pushed onward with my cart, didn't look back, and sure as hell didn't wait for a response.

I haven't seen them since but I can't say I haven't thought about them. Of course, I go to that store now only very early in the morning because I know they'll never be there at that hour. I doubt they could get out of bed before 10 a.m. on any weekend day. For them, it was always a good time to drink, but on Friday and Saturday nights, the time was especially right. My resentment refuses to fade. Why did I have to run into them? Not that everything was peachy before the encounter, but I most certainly wasn't driven to whiskey.

After the encounter, I went to see the gravesite of my real parents, my only parents as far as I am concerned. I needed a reminder of where I really came from, something to make me forget my once-wretched upbringing, and the fosters. As sad as it was to lose my parents, standing at their graves and speaking to them always makes me feel better. Besides, as time has gone by, the sting of their death has softened some. Never easy, mind you, but easier.

I took my usual seat on the bus near Charlie, the driver. We know each other well enough that there was no hiding my less than pleasant disposition. The odd hour of my ride was a dead giveaway too. I'm predictable, if nothing else, and I rarely go off chart.

"You doing okay, Jackson? Been a while since I've taken you uptown like this. Your eyes look like your soul is twisting and turning in there." Charlie repeatedly glanced to the big mirror above his head to keep an eye on me.

"I'm okay, I guess. Thanks for asking. Just wicked people always finding a way to ooze through the cracks." I rubbed my neck to try and ease the tension. I could feel a knot forming that I would need to put a hot pack on later.

"Let me take a guess. You see them?"

Damn he's good, I thought. Knows me better than I know myself. For a second, I wasn't sure if he was my bus driver or my friend. Perhaps he's both. Not perhaps. He drives the bus I ride and he is my friend. Why can't he be both? No reason at all.

"Yeah. They're just not nice people and it burns me up sometimes. Ran into them at the store. We barely even said ten words to each other, but it was like I had just heard ever nasty word she had ever said to me. Kind of like a thirty-foot wave just knocked me on my ass."

I turned my attention out the window of the bus. I saw all the buildings and cars and people as we buzzed by, yet I didn't really see anything except the fosters standing in front of my shopping cart. And I didn't really feel anything either, except the pit in my stomach and the nearly uncontrollable urge to turn and bolt to the furthest point on Earth away from them. How far away is Antarctica? I could deal with the cold. Joke. I'm sure Vostok is beautiful in the summer. I had read about the research base there in a National Geographic Magazine when I was younger and hanging out at the library. Coldest recorded temperatures on the planet. I'd never run into those pricks there, that's for damn sure.

"You're a better person than that, Jackson. Good and bad people will come into your life, nuttin' you can do about that. But you're a grown man now and you got the choice."

"What choice? I never know when I'll run into them. I don't know how to keep the anger from bubbling up."

"They can't hurt you anymore, just remember that. The past happened, you can't change that, but you're free now. Life is too short to be a prisoner to them now."

"But I feel like they didn't learn their lesson, like justice hasn't been served. They got off scot-free for what they did to me. I feel like I want to cause them pain so they know how I feel, or at least have them acknowledge how hurtful they were to me. They've never once fessed up to their bull-crap."

"Justice may not come in the way you want it to. God will take care of that. Besides, the best way for you to punish them is to be free and succeed in life, in spite of what they did. They hurt you but you overcame. That's a lesson for everyone, you, me, and them. Being the opposite of them, not falling into the cycle, that's justice my friend. Best kind there is."

The bus slowed and screeched to a stop.

"This your spot, Jackson. Remember what I said."

I got up from my seat and headed to the doors. Just before I hopped off the last step, I turned and faced Charlie.

"Thanks, Charlie. I really appreciate your insight. It means a helluva lot to me."

He nodded and I waved.

After exiting the bus about half a mile from the entrance to the cemetery, I walked solemnly with my hands inside the front pouch of my hoodie, my head down, staring at my feet hitting the sidewalk and pulling back up again to take each step.

I walked the long winding gravel path through the old tombstones and even older trees. Half-way in and twenty paces to the right are my parent's markers. They are beautiful; charcoal colored granite with white lettering.

I sat on the ground in front of them, directly centered, and said all the things I needed to, asked the profound questions I always do, and kept still for a while waiting and hoping to somehow hear their voices with all the answers. I can't remember now what their voices sounded like and that makes my heart ache. I'm not sure I can even remember what they look like either. I know their faces, but I've come to believe that is only because of the photos I still have, not from my actual memory of their living faces. Time erodes the past, I've found, like the tide washing away all the beachgoer's footprints from the day. Only when we return to the beach are new impressions made, otherwise it remains smooth, no trace of anyone ever having been there. Sadly, I can never walk on that sand again. They are long gone and never coming back.

I keep my apartment dark when I get home. It suits my mood. I decide to just get into bed, the booze and pills my only company for the night. I really hate brooding. I think this alcohol was a mistake. It's making me even more depressed. I take another drink anyway, this time a super-sized gulp, hoping it will finally just knock me out.

I sit in a daze, in the pitch black, my head spinning. I grip the bottle of pills in my left hand like I'm hanging on for dear life to a tree during a tornado. My knuckles actually hurt. The booze bottle rests loosely between my legs. I have no idea what happened to the cap.

Childhood memories keep flowing in and out of my head, each taking a swing at my psyche and leaving me bruised. As they pass through, I unconsciously utter words like: bitch, loser, cunt, stupid, moron, asshole, worthless, shithead. I'm not even sure anymore whether all these words are ones used against me or ones I use against myself.

I'm at a point where I just don't want to breathe anymore. That's the only way I can stop thinking about how pitiful my life is, what an idiot I am, how isolated I feel in the world. My adulthood was supposed to come with freedom and peace, but I don't feel free or amity. I want out. I hate my life. I miss my mom and dad. They would know what to say, but they can't say anything, they're dead. Maybe it would just be easier to join them.

I ponder the thought to end all thoughts. I have whiskey and I have sleeping pills. I washed the idea from my mind earlier in the evening but now I wonder if I didn't really know all along what would end up happening.

I keep hold of the bottle with my left hand and attempt to remove the cap with my right. My coordination falters. I try and remember which type of lid it had: push down and twist, or hold the two side tabs and turn. Shit. I need to turn on the light. I reach over and press the lamp button with the bottom of the pill bottle. I feel moisture on my left leg and realize the JD has spilt a little, so I set the pills on the nightstand and grab the whiskey bottle. I fumble around the bed and find the cap, twisting it on before tossing the booze near my feet.

When I turn to try again with the pills, I see them sitting on top of the flyer I had pulled from the bus stop, the one regarding a crisis hotline. What are the fucking odds? My head is still revolving like a broken record player going too fast, making Led Zeppelin sound like Alvin and the Fucking Chipmunks.

I release a huge sigh and tilt my head back. "What the hell am I doing?" Tears fall from the corners of my eyes. In anger, I expel my hostility toward the ceiling, "Why do I let them do this to me? I didn't do anything wrong! Fuck! Fuck! Fuck!" I put my head down and break into an all-out wail and cry fit. For a time, the sobbing is uncontrollable and I choke some because I barely get any air in as I go on and on.

The alcohol must have let down my inhibitions. I'm actually thinking about calling the hotline. I even give myself a pep-talk. "It's totally anonymous. They won't know my name. I'll just give'em a fake one anyway. I assume they're professionals, maybe they know something I don't. What the hell."

I pick up my cell phone from the nightstand and the flyer from underneath the pills, knocking them to the floor in the process. Through a foggy mind and foggier eyes, I somehow swipe the phone awake.

"You've reached the crisis hotline. This is Lisa speaking and I'm here to help you in any way I can. Can I have your name?"

I remain silent for a few seconds. Lisa was my mother's name. That's so strange. I ponder whether I should just hang up or not, but I finally relent. "I'm Jackson." I swallow hard, fighting my emotions and trying to keep my head clear. The booze has really done a number on my ability to focus. I'm scared, however, so I think the adrenaline is helping me concentrate. Shit. I was supposed to use a fake name. Well, too late now.

"Hello, Jackson. I'm glad you called. Again, I'm Lisa. I take it you're having some trouble tonight? Would you care to share with me how you're feeling right now?"

"I ... I ... I'm in a lot of pain, and I'm lonely, I guess. I don't know what the point of all this is anymore. I'm just tired of the fight. So tired."

"I get that. Life is a bitch sometimes. Right? I've had that feeling. You said you were in pain. Is that pain emotional pain or physical pain?" she asks.

She has a sweet voice, very calming. She sounds pretty, not that a voice necessarily has anything to do with physical beauty, it just creates a certain picture in my mind.

"Both. I've been having some ... digestive problems and some back pain in recent weeks. Hard time sleeping." I intentionally avoid talking about the emotional pain even though I know she would much rather have me discuss that.

"Have you seen a doctor about your health issues?"

"No. Can't really afford it."

"I know from personal experience how stressful it can be to have chronic pain and medical issues. It can easily drive a person mad. You know what I mean?"

"I do."

Lisa is doing a great job in trying to relate to me. I can see the techniques being plied to make me feel comfortable. Salespeople use some of the same methods to connect to their customers. In this case, just talking to someone is already helping me calm down. My mood is still shaky though, and the images of my horrid past are now just pissing me off.

"So, Jackson, are your health problems the thing that is causing you to reach out tonight, or is there something bigger going on? Remember, I'm here to help you. You can tell me anything and I won't judge you, I won't berate you. I just want to make sure you're okay. Are you okay? Are you thinking about doing something ... drastic?"

Wow. She doesn't pull any punches. Let's just get right to the me killing myself part. I see the bottle of pills and wonder if I even have the balls to swallow them. I seriously doubt it. I'm way too chicken-shit. But then again, I had the backbone enough to buy them, and here I am on the phone with Lisa, our friendly neighborhood don't kill yourself call-center girl. I feel like an idiot.

"I don't know. Maybe."

"What were you planning on doing? Let's just talk it out. Maybe we can figure out a path that leads to a better choice."

"Nothing. I don't know."

"What were you planning on doing? Let's just talk it out. Maybe we can figure out a path that leads to better choice."

I must be drunker than I think. I could swear she just asked me the same question twice. Weird.

I don't want to answer but I give in, just so I can get off the phone quicker. "Well, I'm a former foster child and I recently bumped into my former foster parents." I'm being a snide ass when speaking about them. I really hate them. "Let's just say, I bailed from their custody the day I turned eighteen. It wasn't a good environment and they made me feel like I was nothing but a big hassle. It didn't help either that both my foster brothers relentlessly tormented me." I change my tone. "Uh! God! They just really piss me off. The more I think about them, the angrier I get."

"I imagine that meeting brought back many bad memories for you. Isn't it amazing how easily we get sucked back in to our past life with even the smallest trigger?"

"Yes it is. And it bites ass! It makes me feel so stupid that I get all jacked up just seeing them."

"Jackson, it's not stupid to have an emotional reaction about them, and you have every right to be mad. No one deserves to be treated in an abusive manner, but it does happen. We all experience tough situations. The question becomes, how will you let it affect you? Will it come to define you as a person? Weak? Depressed? Angry? Or will you let it empower you? Let it be an example of how not to act and live. And in spite of another person's behavior, you can use it to thrive and be successful, strong, happy, and proud of yourself ... or you can do the exact opposite. Do you think you can take the positive position, Jackson?"

"I don't know how. I'm such a loser. I have no real friends. I'm too fat to even have a chance with a woman. I do admit, I am good at my job but that place is small time." Here I am again, finding a way to diminish the one good thing about my life. Typical.

"That, in itself, is something you should be using as an example of your success. You found a job that you're good at and that you enjoy. You do enjoy it?"

"Oh yeah, I love it. I'm a natural with computers. And if I'm going to be honest, I'm pretty much the backbone of that place. I just wish I had the same confidence in my personal life. Outside of work, I feel so out of place, and I'm growing weary of the constant battle and the feeling of being alone. I'm starting to see the world in such a dark way, and ... I don't know. I just don't know what to do."

"Well, like I've said, the world is full of darkness and hardship, but always remember, there are bright spots too, and wonderful things to do and see and experience. You just have to open yourself up to see them. It's easy to get caught up in a downward spiral of negativity, and there is only one way to get out of it. You have to consciously choose to break the cycle."

"How can I do that? Where would I even begin?"

"You are part of the way there already. You have a great job that you love and excel at. That goes a long way in creating your own happiness. Now, your personal life is another issue, but obviously you have acknowledged it's a problem and that you need help with it. That has culminated in us having this conversation tonight. Whether or not you realize it, you are reaching out for help because you want things to be better, you just don't know how to do it. That's a giant step in the right direction. Sometimes just talking to someone, anyone, can help bring things into perspective, allowing a person to see the bigger picture. Does that make sense?"

"I guess so. I just find it hard to share things with people. It's just not my thing. I internalize. I wouldn't know how to break that, even if I wanted to."

"Let me make a suggestion, something for you to try for a while, to see if it helps."

"Okay."

"Whenever you're feeling particularly bad about something - how lonely you are, or your foster family - go for a walk. It can help clear your mind and refocus your thoughts. And while you're out there, look for the good and beautiful things that exist in the world. Find a flower garden or a park, children playing, an old oak tree to sit and read under."

"A pretty girl to talk to?" I ask sardonically.

"Yes, Jackson. Even a pretty girl to talk to. Why not?"

"That seems a little too simple to me. Go look for some pretty flowers?" I question, sarcasm still dripping from my tongue.

"I know it sounds trivial and maybe a little goofy, but it might just be that you're holding on to all negative aspects of your life, and you haven't left enough room for the good things. Even if you don't have very many positive things, your life has no space for them to enter when they come along. Think of your life as an over-cluttered garage, just chock full of years and years of junk: old boxes, Christmas decorations, broken bicycles, whatever. You've decided to get a new car but quickly realize you can't because you have no place to park it. The only way that new, shiny red car is going to happen for you is if you take the time to throw out the crap, allowing some space in your life for something amazing. You get me?"

"I do. That makes sense."

"Just start there and soon you'll be on your way. No harm in trying."

I sit silent, contemplating everything Lisa has said. Luckily, I'm not so drunk that I don't understand. I just hope I remember all this in the morning. I sniff to let her know I am still on the line.

"How do you feel about all this, Jackson?"

"I feel drunk and stupid and useless."

"How do you feel about all this, Jackson?"

What the hell? She did it again. Does she not believe me?

"I feel like an idiot and a moron."

"How do you feel about all this, Jackson?"

I'm either hearing things or I'm dreaming, like a waking dream, one that you can almost kind of control, even rewind various parts of it to get a do-over. I suppose I'll try again.

"I feel better. Thank you. Maybe I did just need someone to talk to." I let out a big sigh. "I just wish I had more courage to make friends and maybe have a relationship. I have these gamer friends but I'm too much of a pansy to meet them in person. I'm scared of what they'll think of me."

"You're pretty much at the bottom of the barrel right now, wouldn't you say? Take a chance, Jackson. What's the worst that could happen? Do you really have any lower to fall? Will each attempt at making your life better succeed? No. Will every person you meet turn into a good friendship? No. But each try will garner more courage for the next round, and before you know it, you'll be right where you want to be. One of those beautiful things in life I mentioned earlier is the special relationships you can have with other people. I know you have had some bad experiences with people you should've been able to trust and love, and they failed you, but not every relationship will fail, and the ones that don't fail are worth more than just about anything in the world. But you have to be open to them. Trust me on that. Take a leap. Don't waste another minute avoiding the minefield, go right through it. It will hurt from time to time, but what you'll gain in the long run will more than make up for it."

"You're so right. What the hell do I have to lose at this point? Worst case scenario, I'm still the lonely, pathetic, loser I've always been." I smirk at my own lack of self-esteem and the degrading nature of my words. There's nothing like deeply ingrained self-deprecation to spoil a conversation.

"I know you feel that way now, but if you give yourself a chance, I think you'll find those words untrue."

"I hope so. I really do. I'm actually getting pretty tired now. I think I need to sleep."

"I'm just going to be bold here, but are you sure you're okay? You're not going to hurt yourself or anything like that? Please don't be insulted. I wouldn't be doing either of us any favors if I didn't ask."

"Nope. Crisis averted, for now. Thanks again. I do feel better. I'm just starting to have trouble keeping my eyes open."

"Good. Just remember what I've said and just try some things out, see where you're at in a few months. If you need help again, even if it's just to talk for a few minutes, feel free to call anytime. Just ask for Lisa."

"Will do, Lisa. Well, I guess that's goodbye then."

"Goodbye, Jackson. And good luck."

"Thanks. Bye." I press END on my phone and take a deep breath. My head is spinning with information and not as much from the alcohol as I might expect.

I toss the cell phone on the nightstand, twist the whiskey bottle cap off one last time, and take three continuous gulps. I wipe my mouth with the back of my free hand and replace the cap before carelessly tossing the bottle on the floor near where the pills had fallen. I flick off the light and lay back on my pillows. I don't even pull the covers up. I try hard to focus on Lisa's voice, that sweet, encouraging voice, but I find no clarity before blacking out.

CHAPTER SIX

I'm running as fast as I can. Ned Jr. and Nick are not far behind me. I keep glancing over my shoulder to see how far back they are, and they're close, refusing to give up. I figure if I just get home I'll be safe. They won't beat me up in front of Ned and Emma; at least I hope they won't.

Then, abruptly, I'm home. I race up the sidewalk, hit the stairs on the front porch two at a time, and throw the door open. I slow to a speed walk as I hunt through the lower floor for Ned or

Emma. The house is quiet and they are nowhere to be found. I start to jog around, searching for parental intervention. I run up the stairs to the second floor of the house where all the bedrooms are located. It's probably not a good idea to rush into their room. Who knows what they might be doing in there, and they will be pissed if I wake them from a nap, but I'm desperate.

I open the door, slowly, watching through the growing crack. Halfway ajar, I can see the bed is empty. Crap. They're not home. Where can they be? At least one of them is always here when we get home from school.

In a flash, I'm standing at the top of the stairs and in the front door walks Ned Jr. followed by Nick, both panting as bad as I was when I first came in. I freeze, unsure what to do. My stomach aches with the pains of the future ass-kicking I feel I am about to receive. They spot me immediately.

Ned Jr. tosses his bag aside and locks a glare on me. The evil hiding inside is apparent in his eyes. The incident at school that began this escapade left my foster brothers rather embarrassed, especially Ned Jr., and red hot angry at yours truly.

For some reason, I just couldn't handle any more of the constant and unwavering verbal abuses I had been sustaining from those jerks, and today was just the day I mustered enough courage to stand up for myself, and for once, turn the tables on them. I may come to regret my decision to trip Ned Jr. in the hallway after classes had let out, payback for him doing the same to me at lunch, making me spill my lunch tray and having to endure the entire cafeteria laughing relentlessly at me. I boiled with rage the rest of the day and could barely focus on my other classes. Middle school is difficult enough with cliques forming and every pubescent child ready to challenge everything. Each action I take will be emblazoned on my permanent record of teenage repute. My tray spillage made the top ten reject moments that year, and a top three in my book. Revenge would be sweet, for all of about ten seconds. I am about to find out the repercussions of my sudden flights of fancy and temporary balls of steel.

I leap ahead and I'm face down on the carpet of my bedroom. Nick is sitting on my bed rifling through my backpack, no doubt searching for something to incinerate or shred. Ned Jr. has a knee firmly planted in my lower back. He grabs my hair and pulls my head back, forcing me to arch my back even more against his knee. The pain is excruciating. He slams my face down into the carpet again but doesn't let go of my hair. I can no longer bear the throbbing in my lower back and the room goes dark.

Hours later, I wake in a strange place and a strange bed. Someone is standing over me. I don't know her. She's wearing pink scrubs and she is messing with the wires and tubes dangling near my left wrist.

"How you feeling, Jackson? You've been through quite an ordeal but you're going to be okay." She places an arm under my pillow and pulls it downward to better support my neck.

"I'm good. What happened?"

Seemingly out of nowhere, my foster mother pops into view.

"I'll tell ya what happened. You and your brothers were horse-assing around and the little wimp got hurt."

Is that the story they've been telling everyone? I think someone's been feeding her a bunch of bull-crap. Figures. Of course, the truth would be too revealing. I stood up for myself for once in my life, the foster brothers chased me home, and then kicked the crap out of me. I do remember that. But I can hear her saying it now. My boys would never do anything like that. They're angels. Boys will be boys.

Give me a break.

"This little incident is gonna cost us a fortune too. Never fails. You're such a damn hassle sometimes. I don't know why I bother. My good Christian nature demands it, I guess."

I see the nurse roll her eyes and I crack a smile knowing I'm not the only one that can see through the bitch's lies. Regardless, my life is going to be hell for months because of this. I hate hospitals, but today I wish I could stay here forever. My so-called home life is anything but homey, more like a living hell.

"Jackson, you're going to be fine. There was some trauma to one of your kidneys, making it very weak. It's no longer functioning at full capacity, but luckily we all have two kidneys, so you shouldn't have any problem. I'll be back shortly to check on you again." She gives me a long smile, a sadness in her eyes for my obviously shitty family situation. I appreciate the sympathy but it's not going to help me. I long for the day I am old enough to move out and be on my own. I'd rather live in a cardboard box under a bridge than spend the rest of my life with the fosters. When I get out of high school, I'm gone.

CHAPTER SEVEN

It's Wednesday, early, and I have a massive headache and hangover. My eyes hurt when I open them more than a squint. I manage to call Henry and let him know I want to take the day off. He makes no fuss and even offers to bring me lunch, which I appreciate but refuse. In truth, the drinking and the emotional crap I'm dealing with are the reason I called in sick.

After hanging up with Henry, I glance at my call log. I puzzle over what I see, or more accurately, what I don't see. The call I made to the hotline is not listed. Did I delete the log after making the call? Nope. Not possible. My phone only allows me to delete calls by the day, not individually, and the ones from early in the day yesterday are still there. What the hell? Did I simply imagine the call? Was it all a dream? Doesn't seem possible.

I search my room for the flyer and find nothing. I clearly remember grabbing the flyer and pulling it from the drawer, but now it's nowhere to be found.

I scratch my head and question the amount of booze I inhaled last night. Man, when I imagine shit, I go big. That was probably the most realistic dream I have ever had, window to the soul and all that. Well, I do give good advice, even if it's to myself, by myself, and for myself. I might have been dangerously close to doing something truly stupid if my inner Lisa hadn't talked me down. Or maybe, the voice of my mother is still somewhere inside me, guiding me. I find comfort in the thought, and my heart swells with love for my mom in a way I've never experienced.

Beyond that, I'm not sure if the alcohol jogged something loose or if it's just a coincidence, but I'm actually feeling significantly better today, at least as far as my lower back and bladder are concerned. I peed like a racehorse when I woke up and the pain in my back has subsided to the point where I can stand up straight when I walk. Two thumbs up for that. Hopefully, I can avoid a dreaded and overpriced trip to the ER.

I leave the whiskey bottle and the pills right where they are on the floor as a reminder of how pathetic I am and just how close I came to being a ghost. And over what? My idiot foster parents? I can't let them win. I'm better than they are and I know it. Clutter. Time to throw out some fucking trash.

I spend the rest of the morning and afternoon running the campaign of my favorite first person shooter. It feels damn good killing some Nazis with a sniper rifle and ultimately saving the world. My only interruption in gaming for the seven hours I spend in front of the TV is the time it takes for me to make and eat a PB and J. My full appetite still hasn't returned, but the sandwich doesn't make me sick, so that's good. For the record, I passed on the soda today, instead opting for good old-fashioned water. It feels good drinking it. I can't remember the last time I just had water, but I will say this sure could save me a lot of money. With the combination of my new raise and the extra dough from not drinking soda, I might just be able to finally afford to buy a used car. Ohhh. The thought of that makes me very happy.

After conquering my game, probably for the seventh or eighth time since I bought it, I'm feeling better but still harboring some anger. The words of Lisa come to mind. I'm well enough that I think I can handle a short walk to help clear my head, so I get dressed in blue jeans, a gray football hoodie, and sneakers, throw my keys and cell phone in my pockets, and head out. I could use some fresh air and change of scenery.

I hit the sidewalk outside my apartment and the smell of the outdoors is intoxicating. I'm not sure if I have a heightened awareness, a result of my amazing but drunken self-talking session, or if it's something else, but I sense what I imagine a prisoner feels when they exit the twenty foot high sliding gate after five years of incarceration: freedom, but with trepidation about the future.

I pull out my phone and check the weather app. Fifty-two degrees is perfect for an afternoon walk on a mostly clear fall day. My mood is improving quickly.

I stroll down the block, going nowhere in particular. I pass the rest of the apartment buildings in my complex and see two men working on the community pool. I assume they are shutting it down for the season, not that I really care. I don't feel comfortable with my shirt off, not with this little pot belly, so I don't swim anymore. I've thought about wearing a tank top while swimming, but I feel like that will just draw even more attention to the fact I'm trying to hide something. Two summers have come and gone with no pool time for me.

I continue to walk for a few blocks just trying to take in all the sights and sounds of the world. The gentle breeze rustles the leaves of every tree I pass, the already fallen ones skittering all around me, all at different stages of the autumn color change. Every once in a while, I stop and breathe as deeply as I can. I focus on the crisp air and the expansion and contraction of my chest. The anger I hold for my foster parents dissipates some, allowing better thoughts to enter. I'm really looking forward to my next gaming session with the crew. I might just try and arrange an in-person meeting. Why not? I've only got up to go, right? One thing I could live without though is the traffic rushing by - it's killing my peaceful nature-loving vibe, but I work hard to filter out that mess.

There's a school up ahead, Harrison Middle School, which lets me know I'm about eight blocks from home. Classes have let out for the day, but there is heavy activity with buses coming and going, parents arriving to pick up their children, and many kids running around the playground. Their laughter and voices brings a smile to my face, the reverse effect it usually has. My childhood was mostly horrible, so any reminder of that puts me in a bad mood. Not today. For the first time that I can remember, I'm not distressed by the sound. If anything, I'm happy they're enjoying their youth rather than me being pissed off about mine.

I approach the fenced area around the school. The baseball diamond at the corner of the schoolyard is empty. I remember the last time I stepped up to the plate. I was in sixth grade and we played kickball for P.E. I stunk at it. I never once got that stupid red ball out of the infield. My budding physical prowess never quite took off.

As I slowly walk the fence line dragging my finger along the chain links, I see a grove of trees just inside the fence, fifteen feet or so past where a left field homerun would sail. As I get a little closer, I can hear the voices of boys playing amongst the coniferous shade. When I get to about forty feet away, I casually stop when I hear what sounds like a whimper of someone in distress. I can see three boys, maybe twelve or thirteen years old, standing over another boy, somewhat smaller, who is sitting on the ground with his knees to his chest like kids do when sitting in the hallway during a tornado drill. I play it cool, pretending my attention lies elsewhere. I position my right ear toward the grove and listen carefully to confirm what I thought I heard.

"Are you gonna cry? You big baby!" says one boy.

"He's a big pussy. Smack him again," says another boy.

"No. Please don't hit me again," begs the boy on the ground. "Please."

My good mood slips away like a penny falling into a deep, dark well. My stomach aches, full of bad memories. I close my eyes and the world around me drowns out with thoughts of my own past breaking through to the surface of my mind.

I'm ten years old and it's been fifteen months since my parents died and just over a year since my foster family took me in. Twelve-year-old Nick and fourteen-year-old Ned Jr. are jumping together on the trampoline in the backyard. They bore quickly. If they are not destroying something, they are not happy.

I sit quietly next to the giant maple tree on the other side of the yard. The sun is out in full force on this humid summer day, and the large canopy of the tree provides a decent amount of shade that is allowing me to stay cool while I read *To Kill a Mockingbird*.

It's two in the afternoon on a Saturday, so no doubt Mr. Buford is in his recliner, barely conscious, cigarette half-smoked in one hand and a nearly empty bottle of cheap whiskey in the other. He spends the work week from dusk until dawn at a concrete company doing intense manual labor, so he does absolutely nothing on the weekends, which includes paying no attention to his sons, or to me. Mrs. Buford is at work. She's been a waitress at a local coffeehouse for most of her adult life. Being in foodservice, she is rarely home much on the weekends, her normal days off being Monday and Tuesday.

To date, the brothers Buford have ignored me for the most part. As rowdy and unpredictable as they are, I can't complain about their lack of attention. The neglect from Mr. and Mrs. Buford is less than ideal, but then again, I haven't felt much like bonding. The loads of time I've had to myself has helped me deal with the absence of my parents. I have taken advantage of social services counseling to discuss my parent's death and how I can deal with it, so I suppose it hasn't been such a big problem.

Over the top-edge of my borrowed paperback book, I see Ned Jr. and Nick bounce off the edge of the trampoline, restless for something new to sate their incurably idle hands. They stand face to face, half turned toward me, whispering about something and pointing occasionally in my direction. I get the sinking suspicion I am about to be involved in their play time. They walk over to me. I ignore them and pretend to read.

"Hey! What's that you're reading?" Ned Jr. demands.

"You wouldn't like it." I keep my face in the book. In my mind, I ask them to go away.

"How do you know? Let me see it," Ned Jr. once again demands. He reaches to grab the book but I feel the presence of his hand and pull it away just time to keep him from it. "Don't be a dickhead! Let me have it!" He forces his way past my guard and gets a hand on the front cover. I pull away again but it's too late. The cover rips off in a straight line just along the spine.

"You idiot! This book doesn't belong to me. And you've ruined it!"

"Oh, don't get your panties in a twist. It's just a book." Ned Jr. looks to his brother.

Nick rolls his eyes. "Don't be such a girl," he says, finally chiming in.

I think about trying to explain to my teacher how I damaged the book he lent me and my eyes well up. I have so much respect for Mr. Hoffman and the very idea of damaging his property after he trusted me with it sickens me.

I rise to my feet and put my hand out. "Give me the cover please. I'm telling Mr. Buford."

"Mr. Buford? You mean dad. And no, you're not. Sit your ass back down!" Nick shoves me with one hand right into my left shoulder sending me backward into the trunk of the tree. The impact bruises my shoulder blade.

"Ouch. That hurt." With the pain, I can no longer hold back the tears.

"Jesus, you big sissy. I barely touched you." He tosses the cover at my feet. "Here's your stupid cover."

For the moment, I leave it there. I can't stop sobbing.

"If you don't stop all that crying, I'm going to hit you twice as hard and take that damn book and throw it in the fire pit. Now shut it!" Nick says. He taps his brother on the arm and they face each other. "Let's go do something else. This is major boring shit."

"What if he tells on us? Dad will be pissed."

"Who's Dad going to believe? Whiney boy here or us?"

"True. Let's ride down to the park and see if Travis wants to do anything," Ned Jr. says, already moving away from me. "Didn't he say he stole some firecrackers from his brother?"

Nick turns back to me with menace in his eyes and says, "We find out you said anything to Dad, you're dead. You hear me you little fucker? Dead!"

With his right hand, he reaches toward the right side of my head and backhands the side of my face, hard enough to sting and leave a red mark. I wince but remain silent. I'm too shocked at the past few minutes to react.

Nick points his finger right at my face, about two inches from my left eye. "And you'll get worse than that if you don't do what we say from now on, you fucking nerd." He shoves my left shoulder, turns, and runs to catch up with Ned Jr.

I sink to the ground, confused about what had just transpired. My full-on crying has stopped but

I'm still sobbing. I wipe away the moisture from both my cheeks. I can't decide which is hurting more, the physical or the emotional. I close my eyes. Up until now, I have been at relative peace in my new home, but now it appears a new level of suck has just entered.

I open my eyes and I'm back at the middle school. The memory of that day with my foster brothers leaves me in a bit of a daze. That was when everything changed for me within that household. Until then, I suffered mostly neglect, which truthfully, I didn't mind since I really just wanted to be left alone, but now the foster brothers had discovered someone to torment and harass, and they took full advantage. I spent most of the following eight years avoiding them at all costs, and not successfully enough.

I try to focus for a minute to bring myself back into the present. Someone honks their horn nearby which snaps me right out of my trance, then I remember why I stopped in the first place: the boys in the grove.

I look to the trees and the three boys are still standing over the fourth, smaller boy. They are taunting him with words like nerd, idiot, sissy, and they kick dirt at him and throw pine cones at him. For about three seconds, I think about intervening but my shaky emotional state forces my feet backward from the fence until eventually I just turn around and jog back home.

I slam the front door shut and plop down on the couch, out of breath and still reliving bits and pieces of that day some nineteen years ago. That walk was supposed to help me gain some clarity and refocus, instead it stressed me out even more. To boot, I'm starting to feel guilty about not helping that kid out. I only wish some adult would have intervened in one of the many times I got bullied. I'm a sissy. I'm a grown ass man and I didn't have the guts to stand up to a couple of middle school punks. What a wimp.

Now all I can think about is that poor kid, lying on the ground, scared out of his life, silently begging for someone like me to help him out, and just like during my childhood, no one ever does. We talk and talk and talk about stepping up and doing what's right, but once again ... we fail. I failed.

My attention turns quickly to the rumbling of my stomach. All the walking and jogging has left me famished. I'm ecstatic to see my appetite return. Hopefully, I can keep down whatever food I decide on.

I get my butt off the couch and walk to the kitchen. I pull all the takeout menus from the drawer next to the fridge and flip through them until one catches my eye, or more accurately, tingles my taste buds.

Number seven on the speed dial. Two rings and the woman handling the counter in the evening answers. She also happens to be the manager.

"Hi, Ja-son. You want usual?" Her thick accent might be difficult for new customers, but I can deduce what she says by only catching a few syllables - a major advantage to being a regular. They know me by my phone number too, so the exchange is usually quick.

"Yep. Oh no, wait." I forgot about my pledge to lay off the soda. "No more Mountain Dew. Just the food."

"Okay. No Mountain Dew. We be there in ten minute. Okay?"

"Okay. Thank you." I hear the click on her end. I'm certain she didn't catch the last words I said.

Ten minutes on the dot and my food arrives. I give my usual twenty percent tip and take the bag into the kitchen. I pull the containers out and align them on the counter as if I'm about to serve a dozen people buffet-style. Unfortunately, it's just me again, as lonely as ever.

I load my plate with white rice, one half topped with beef and broccoli and the other half with breaded sweet and sour chicken chunks. I don't actually eat the neon pink sauce but I love those deep-fried chicken pieces. I also tear the corner off a soy sauce packet and hit everything on the plate with a spritz. I pour a glass of water and grab my plate. I put on the Science Channel and a show about black holes and dark matter to watch while I eat. I have no idea what happens on the show for the first ten minutes as I'm too busy inhaling my food like I haven't eaten in days. In truth, I guess I haven't really eaten much, and what I have managed to eat, I threw back up.

After I finish eating every last scrap of food from my plate, I decide to take the opportunity to re-watch one of my favorite movies - *Back to the Future*. I bought the trilogy on Blu-ray over the summer and have yet to crack it open. I clean up my dinner mess, strip down to my underwear, and pop the first disc in the player. I turn off the lights and just relax while I enjoy underdogs Marty and George McFly taking on the bully in their lives, and in the end, they each get their girl. If only I could be so lucky.

The boy in the schoolyard crosses my mind a few times as the evening wears on. I deeply regret not getting involved and I promise myself I will not make that mistake again, should the occasion arise. I have a gaming night tomorrow after work, so I'll chat with my online buds about it, just to see what they think I should have done. I'm pretty sure I know the answer.

CHAPTER EIGHT

Work was a breeze. Carlos had taken advantage of the opportunity to prove himself and did an outstanding job keeping the train rolling while I was out sick. We make a great team and it should allow ACME to take on tons more clients. Henry is just glad I am feeling better and back in action, and so am I.

Whatever my illness was, it seems to have subsided. I've managed to eat several times without it coming back up and the pain in my back is down to a mild annoyance. I have my suspicions that the ridiculous amount of soda I drink has been the culprit all along. Water has become my thing now. I'm carrying a bottle around with me everywhere I go. Yes, I'm now like everyone else on the water craze, just five years late to the party. Well excuse me.

I'm in a very good mood after just about the worst week of my life, at least in recent memory. But it's Thursday evening and that means one thing – a scheduled game night with my peeps. I look forward to that time like a kid knowing the next day is the family trip to Disneyworld - nervous and excited. Each day of my life seems to exist as nothing more than a countdown to my next gaming session. A pathetic way to live, no doubt, but it's all I've got going for me right now, so I'll take it.

I'm skipping dinner tonight since Henry bought pizza for the staff today, but I did pop over to the convenience store before coming home to pick up a box of chocolate donettes and a bag of corn chips - munchies and crunchies for gameplay. I'm sure they'll taste better with the water I'll be drinking instead of my usual Dew. Now that I think about it, what a disgusting combination to have endured. On second thought, why haven't I ever thought to have ice cold milk with my donuts? That's a natural combination but it has never crossed my mind until now. I blame the soda addiction. Yes. Damn you, soda.

I check the time in the right-hand corner of my laptop screen: 5:57 p.m. Just a few more minutes and it will be go time. I'm sitting in bed again tonight, laptop on my thighs, a box of donuts resting comfortably by my left hip, the open bag of chips on the other. I type in my username and password.

Online Conversation before starting the game –

RejectGuy99:   Check check

2NE1-KPopper: 1 ... 2 1 ... 2. What up playa?

RejectGuy99:   Oh gawd! I've been sick all week. Feeling better now though. How's classes?

1LonelyGurl: Hello boys. Hows things?

2NE1-KPopper: College is kickin my azzz. Calculus sucks

1LonelyGurl: Ur only a couple weeks into the semester and ur already hurting KPop? That's not a good sign. Maybe RG can tutor you? :-)

ScoobyDont69: Evening lady and gentlemen. Weekend almost here

RejectGuy99: I thought all Asians were good at math?

2NE1-KPopper: Whoa!!!! Take ur white hood off RG

RejectGuy99: Sorry. Waz that racist?

1LonelyGurl: You guys r ridiculous. Good evening Scoob. u wearing a tuxedo or something? So formal

2NE1-KPopper: I wuz kidding bro. We Asians do usually kill at math, I got bad genes.

;-) Hey Scoob!

ScoobyDont69: Nope. Jus being obnoxious. Taking the boy on a fishing trip this weekend. Looking forward to it

RejectGuy99: :-) I could help u KPop. No problem with math

1LonelyGurl: Sounds fun Scoob. I haven't fished since I was a kid

2NE1-KPopper: I might take u up on that RG. My GPA is gonna take a major hit. I need at least a B for that class. BTW-glad ur feeling better

RejectGuy99: Thanks guys. I wanted to ask you all something, kinda serious

ScoobyDont69: What's up RG? Everything ok?

1LonelyGurl: RG – ask away

RejectGuy99: Well, I was walking near a school this week and I came across three boys picking on another smaller boy. It kinda upset me

1LonelyGurl: Oh no. I really hate bullies. What'd ya do?

2NE1-KPopper: Big guys with little dicks, always picking on us smaller dudes. NOT COOL. What happened?

ScoobyDont69: That kind of behavior really upsets me. Did you report it?

RejectGuy99: That's just it. I froze. I did nothing. Actually, it brought back a lot of difficult memories for me. I panicked and turned and left like a big chicken. I feel stupid. And bad for the kid. Should I have intervened?

1LonelyGurl: YES! U absolutely should have stepped in. We can't let that stuff happen. I take it you dealt with some of that as a kid RG?

RejectGuy99: I did not report it. I wish I had. I just froze.

:-(

And yes LG, I've had my fair share of getting pushed around

2NE1-KPopper: Should have went over and handled dem punks. Ur a grown ass man. Handle ur business

ScoobyDont69: My son reported a bully when he was a freshman and didn't regret it for one second and it put that kid on the radar so he couldn't do it anymore. We gotta stand up against this stuff

1LonelyGurl: I agree with Scoob

RejectGuy99: I'm glad I asked you guys about it. I won't be silent the next time. Hopefully there won't be a next time, but if there is, I'll do the right thing. Thanks guys

2NE1-KPopper: Bust 'em up RG :-)

ScoobyDont69: Good. Enough is enough. Everybody ready to play?

1LonelyGurl: Definitely ready. And don't be too hard on yourself RG. Live and learn. Next time, you'll do the right thing

2NE1-KPopper: Let's play!

RejectGuy99: Will do. And Hell Yeah! Let's do this damn thing

CHAPTER NINE

Bus riding tip number three: Don't get too distracted while riding, especially when the driver is a substitute. My usual guy, Charlie, knows where I get off. Fred, however, has no idea who the hell I am, so as I flip through an A+ certification book trying to brush up on a few PC hardware things on the ride, I miss my stop and end up getting off ten blocks away from home. At least I know where I am. I'm just going to have to hoof it.

I'm off a little early as the workload for the week was light, so Henry sent everyone home at 2:30, staying behind himself until close just to make sure someone was there to man the desk and the phone. The rest of us bolted like someone started a fire, pulled the alarm, and told everyone there's free chocolate cake in the parking lot. Getting out of work at that hour on a Friday is a rare treat, no doubt, so no one questioned, no one barked, no one even looked Henry in the eye. Meghan even asked me to pinch her to make sure she wasn't in dreamy-dreamland, then we all ran out of the building like it was the last day of school.

After a few hundred feet of walking, I realize the middle school is just up ahead where my failure from a few days ago took place. I get a knot in my stomach instantly, but I do feel more confident after the pep talk from my fellow gamers. And wouldn't you know it, school let out a little while ago. With any luck, I'll just walk on by and won't see or hear anything. Who am I kidding? I'm not the least bit lucky.

I approach the schoolyard from the opposite direction and from the other side of the street as I had before. I walk with conviction trying hard not to look at the tree line as I pass. To my surprise, my heart is racing. What the hell am I so anxious about? The odds of those stupid kids being there again and to be doing the same thing are remote, at best. My curiosity bests me when I get just past the grove and I sneak a peek. Phew. Nobody is hiding in there. I breathe again.

I reach the corner and hit the crosswalk button. My eyes follow the traffic and watch the red flash, but I purposely avoid looking to the school again. After a few seconds, I cannot resist the temptation to look one last time before I cross the street. Damn my nosiness.

On the other side of the fifteen foot tall backstop fence are two long, aluminum dugout benches. Sitting on the very end of the bench closest to the corner of the fence is the messy haired boy I had seen being harassed by the three other boys just two days ago. I am relieved not to see anyone else near him, but not a moment passes when out of the corner of my eye I spot the three bullies approaching from down the third base line. The boy doesn't see them coming, his head in a book.

"Jesus," I say, but not loud enough that anyone would hear unless they were standing right next to me. "Why does this kid keep isolating himself in areas where he's an easy target?" I put my hand over my mouth as I speak so nearby people don't think I'm talking to myself. "If he just stayed near the building, he'd be out of harm's way, but no, he has to disappear to a place where no one can help him. He's a damn sitting duck."

The electronic green hand appears on the other side of the street but I ignore it. I feel I have no choice but to stick around and make sure the kid is all right. I'm not going to make the same mistake again. If they mess with him, no matter how scared I feel, I am going to butt-in.

For the moment, I stay on the corner, eyes fixed on the bullies who are now standing right in front of the bench where the boy is reading. They say something to him, the taller one kicking dirt at him, but I can't hear the words. The boy doesn't budge, instead keeps his eyes in the book, I'm sure quietly praying they get struck by lightning.

The blond haired one of the band of misfits raises his voice and I assume repeats himself. This time I can hear some of the words: ... talking to ... idiot. What ... you deaf? ... that ... reading? ... nerd!

I can see this isn't going anywhere good, so I press the other button on the pole next to me and face the crosswalk leading to the baseball diamond. It's go time.

I impatiently look to the stoplights to catch them changing but they are taking forever. Meanwhile, the shortest of the three boys, the one with tanned skin and pitch black hair, grabs the book and tosses it down the first base line. The boy on the bench stands up in protest but is shoved back down by the blond.

I'm tapping the fingers of my right hand on the top of my left hand, tired of waiting for the damn light to change, so I make a decision and bolt into the street. I easily make it over the first two lanes and into the median. Cars are continually rounding the corner and cutting in front of me but I have no time.

The boy on the bench is now being tussled about by all three of the others. The blonde suddenly decides to get even more physical. He grabs the boy on the side of his head and forces him sideways onto the bench, pressing his cheek hard against the metal. He is helpless. Outnumbered, he does little to resist.

I'm pissed now. "Fuck it." I jump into the first lane of the two in front of me. So far, so good. A car turns the corner and races past me and as soon as the rear bumper clears, I make a run for it. Another car flies around the bend and slams on the brakes before laying on the horn. My knees lock and the middle of my body bends me into the shape of the letter c. The driver's side headlight of the Toyota SUV is just four inches from my leg. I wave at the driver to acknowledge my mistake and to let him know that I was okay. I step to the sidewalk and try to catch my breath. I then remember why I had acted so stupid in the first place.

The near miss in the street has drawn the attention of the bullies and they temporarily halt the abuse of the other kid. The three of them look right at me like I'm some dumbass who had just about got himself killed, which I guess I had. The blonde keeps his hand on the boys head, pinned to the bench.

I walk right up to the fence and breathing a little heavy say, "What the hell do you think you're doing? Let that kid go." I'm proud of myself. I sound confident and authoritative.

"What are you going to do about it? Loser!" says the blonde, clearly the ring leader.

"I tell you what I'm going to do. I'm going to come around this fence and pummel you little shits if you don't stop messing with him. I saw you the other day too, over in those trees." I point. "I know who all of you are and I'm going to report you to the school if you don't leave him the fuck alone. Now get the hell outta here!" I wait to see their reaction. They seem puzzled but leery. They don't act fast enough for my liking. "Now!"

The blonde releases his hand with one last shove on the boy's head. They casually walk back the way they came, mumbling incoherently, glancing back on occasion to see if I'm gone. I'm not.

I walk down to the opening in the fence, enter, and walk over to meet the boy. He is standing near the bench. He has his eyeglasses in his hand, the left arm of them bent out of shape from getting his head smashed into the bench. He just stares at them; maybe trying to figure out what he can do to fix them, or maybe wondering how he was going to explain them to his parents. Either way, he's terrified.

"Hey kid. You all right?"

"They broke my glasses. And they tossed my book." He points to where it landed.

I jog over and grab it, then walk back and hand it him. It's in good shape except for the dirt.

He inspects it, putting it close to his face. He must be extremely near-sighted. Once satisfied, he slumps down to the bench and places the book at his side. He checks his glasses again and gently twists the misshapen arm with little luck in returning it to proper form. He carefully places them on his face anyway, the left side resting below his ear rather than on it. He finally looks at me.

"Thanks," the boy says timidly.

"You're welcome." He seems like a sweet kid and I feel even worse now for not getting involved the other day. He reminds me of me at that age: always reading, kind of a geek, and small for his age, though I don't actually know how old he is, just basing that assumption on the size of the other boys.

"So ... you saw them messing with me the other day too?"

"Yeah. Sorry about that. I kind of panicked, didn't know how to react. That kind of thing happened to me a lot when I was young too. By the way, I'm Jackson. What's your name?"

"Cooper, but my friends call me Coop. Well, at least they used to, before I moved here."

"Nice to meet you, Coop. I take it this is your first year at this school?"

"Yes. Not off to great start. Already got dingleberries like those guys giving me crap. My old school was a Magnet school, so most of the kids were smart and nerdy like me. I never got picked on, that's for sure."

"That sucks. Sorry." I can see Coop is relaxing. His shoulders are less tense and his hands have stopped shaking. Ditto for me. "You waiting for your mom or dad to pick you up from school?"

"My mom, yes. She gets off work at four, so I have to just wait here. I figured if I came all the way over here to the baseball field those guys wouldn't notice me. I'm not that lucky. Thanks again for scaring them away."

"You and me both kid. There ain't no luck for guys like us except bad luck. I'm just glad I was here. You probably need to tell your mom or a teacher about those guys. Don't tolerate that crap. There's no reason for it."

"I don't wanna cause any trouble or be a big tattle-tale."

"But you need to. If guys like that are allowed to continue, we're giving them a clear message saying it's okay. It's most definitely NOT okay."

"You're right."

"It's different now from when I was a young. Nowadays, kids are encouraged to speak up. And hey, either you do it or I'm gonna. If *you* do, at least it'll seem like you're fighting your own battles."

"So, you used to get hassled too? What did you do?"

"I grew up and moved out. I made the mistake of not getting help. It was a little different. It was my own foster brothers that bullied the hell out of me for like eight years, and my foster parents didn't give a shit." I wince. "Sorry for the language. Hell, I'm sure you've heard far worse."

I pull my cell phone out of my pocket to check the time. It's a few minutes after four. Coop's mom will be here soon enough, so I can probably leave. Plus, I don't want her to see some random guy sitting here with her son. She might get the wrong impression.

"Well ... your mom will be here shortly and I don't think those boys are coming back, so I'm going to take off." I get to my feet.

"Okay. Thanks, Jackson. Maybe I'll see you around?" He looks up at me and my heart melts. I see in his eyes the same isolation I often feel, with no real friends, no one that sees the full depth of his being - a soul walking alone in the world.

I smile a bittersweet smile, one with pain but also with hope. "Yeah, you'll see me around. I live at the Orchard Park Apartments over on Fifth Street." I point down the road in the direction I'll be heading. "I work at ACME computers across town. You ever hear of it?"

"Nope. We haven't been in town long, so I don't know where anything is yet."

"Oh. Well, if you're interested in computers at all, maybe I can show you a few things about building them."

"I love computers but I've never built one before. Sounds cool."

"All right then, Coop. I'm heading home. Keep your chin up kid ... and tell somebody what those idiots have been doing to you. You'll thank me later."

"I will."

I nod and put my hand on his shoulder, then give it a couple of taps and head off. When I'm at the corner waiting for the stoplight, I look back and see Coop still sitting there, stuffing the book into his bag. We wave to each other. I turn just in time for the hand signal to change to green and I'm off for home.

My walk is quick. The time flies by with Coop's sad face on my mind and the conversation reeling over and over through my brain. I still can't believe I had the cojones to step in and help the poor kid out. The more I think about it, the more I want to puke. I don't get worked up easily, but apparently when I do, the volcano erupts. This was the second time in recent memory that I have stood up and demanded change. Will the real Jackson Reed please step forward? The super confident, alien version of Jackson can now return to the mother ship and head back to his home planet near Alpha Centauri.

CHAPTER TEN

After a couple of weeks of smooth sailing, at least as far as workload is concerned, this week is starting off with a bang. Around this time of year, a month or so after school is back in session, we get an influx of laptops that high school and college students have somehow already managed to muck up. Most of the time it's a virus, a Trojan, malware, etc... On occasion, the wireless card or hard drive has gone on the blitz. We are authorized to service warranties for most computer manufacturers, so that multiples the flood ten-fold, easy.

By 11:30 I'm exhausted. I feel much like how a professional athlete must feel at training camp after a long off-season. I had to quit working on hardware before 9 a.m. I got fed up after dropping about twenty of those damn tiny laptop screws on the floor. Carlos traded me stations so I could do less hardware damage, allowing me to work on software installs and updates. Click OK ... wait. Click CONTINUE ... wait. Reboot will begin in 10 ... 9 ... 8 ... All boring but harmless, not many ways for me to botch it up.

I'm sitting here staring at the screen of my work laptop, lost in thought about a million things, yet nothing at all, when I hear the front door entrance bell. I don't usually even notice it anymore, like the white noise of my box fan while I sleep, but the sound catches my attention this time. I'm on the verge of taking my lunch break anyway, so I pull the laptop screen down and push away from the table. Just after I rise from the chair and turn to begin walking out of the shop, Meghan appears at the doorway.

"Hey J-Dog, you have a visitor," she says seductively.

Visitor? What am I, in prison? Feels like it sometimes. It is weird though. I don't think anyone has ever paid me a visit at work before. Hell, I don't know anybody. This is definitely weird.

"Meghan, I know it's fun and I'm not upset or anything, but can we leave the whole J-Dog thing behind? Call me Jackson. I feel like a gangster when you guys call me that." I push my chair in and head toward her, curious as to who is here to see me.

"Okay. Sorry. I didn't know it bothered you. We've been calling you that forever. Why haven't you said anything before?" She moves aside to let me pass.

"I don't know. I'm just ... over it. No biggie."

"Ok," she says as she follows me to the front line.

I go to the center of the area behind the counter as if to speak to a customer rather than a visitor, mostly by instinct. Like I said, I don't believe I've ever had one at work.

I face the woman standing there and put on my best ACME service smile. She's kind of cute, maybe late twenties, with gorgeous green eyes and super long, reddish-brown hair in a thick braid resting on her left shoulder. Her attire - a simple white blouse and navy blue slacks, suggesting she works a white collar job, probably here on her lunch break. I expect to see her carrying a laptop or other electronic device; instead she's holding an opaque food storage container with a blue lid.

"I'm Jackson. What can I do for you?"

"Hi ... um ... we've never met. I'm Kelly Dansbury. I believe you met my son, Cooper."

"Oh ... yeah. Coop. Good kid," I say with fake indifference. The last thing in the world I expected today was Coop's mom showing up at work. I hope she's not here to give me shit. My day has been tough enough already. "Is everything okay?"

"More than okay, actually. He told me what you did for him and about those boys picking on him. I just wanted to come down and say thank you for getting involved."

I look away with embarrassment and see Henry, Carlos, and Meghan all standing at the doorway to the back area, watching and listening intently. I shot them a glare as if to say bugger off. Henry complies and hustles them off to the break room.

"Well, they were all bigger than Coop and I felt bad for him. I used to get grief like that when I was his age too, so... His glasses got kinda messed up. He was pretty upset about it. How's he doing?"

"He's doing much better. We got his glasses fixed on Saturday. He's blind as a bat without them. Here." Kelly places the container on the counter and slides it toward me. "They're chocolate chip. I hope that's okay?"

"You didn't have to do that. It was really no trouble. But heck yeah chocolate chip are okay." I smile wide and am already thinking about the milk I'm going to need to buy to go with them. Yummy. "Thank you so much."

"It's quite all right. And thank you. I don't know what you two talked about but he kept going on and on about you, and that from a boy who internalizes a lot. He really took a liking to you."

"I'm flattered, really, but I only did what anyone would have done in that situation."

"Maybe. But it wasn't just anyone, it was you. Our Hero. So enjoy the cookies and before I head back to the office, I want to invite you over for dinner."

I casually put a hand up and mouth the word "no" to suggest it wouldn't be necessary, but she doesn't give me enough time to refuse.

"I insist. Cookies are fun but dinner is the least we can do. I don't think you realize the impact you've had on Coop. You've made quite an impression and it would mean so much if he could see you again. And it would mean a lot to me too." She lays the puppy dog eyes on me. "Pleeeeeease."

The words of Lisa come to mind. In order to find the good things in life, I will need to take a chance sometimes. What do I have to lose? It's just dinner and it's not like she's asking me to adopt the kid.

"I'd be happy to come over. Thank you," I relent, a baby step, hopefully in the right direction in my new anti-lonely campaign.

"Oh good. Coop will be so excited. He never thought he would see you again. Do you have a favorite kind of food? I can make anything you want, just name it."

"I'd eat just about anything. Whatever is easy for you. I don't want to be any trouble."

"Absolutely no trouble. I make a mean meatloaf and mashed potatoes. How's that sound?"

"Ooo. That sounds great. I can't remember the last time I had a home-cooked meal. Can I bring some kind of bread or something?"

"Please do. That'll be perfect." Kelly checks her watch and gets that I'm going to be late look on her face. "I really need to get back to work or I'm going to get in trouble."

I pull my phone out of my pocket and bring up a note taking app. "Okay. Let me get your address."

"That would be helpful, huh? It's 18901 Gaslight Lane. It's actually not too far from here, maybe two miles east. Are you available next Friday evening, say ... around 6 p.m.?"

"Um ... yeah, that should be fine. I'll just take the bus straight from here and it'll be good."

"Oh. I didn't realize you didn't have a car. Let me pick you up then. It would just be easier."

"Yeah, I'm working on the car thing. I think I can finally afford to get one soon. Just trying to save a little money for a down payment. You sure it's okay? I don't really mind the bus. I've been taking it for years." I feel guilty now. This woman has already gone out of her way to make and bring me cookies and has offered to make me dinner, now she's willing to give me a ride to her house.

"It's more than okay. The least I can do. I get off work around four, have to pick up Coop, then I can swing by and get you. Would it be easier to pick you up here or from your home? I'm fine either way." She looks to her watch again. "I really got to go."

"You can pick me up from here. That'll be great. Thank you. You better head out. I don't want you to be late on account of me. Thanks for the cookies."

"Great. I'll see you then. Thanks again. It was great to meet you." She steps backward away from the counter.

I wave a simple goodbye and she does the same as she turns and leaves the store.

I wait a few seconds before I move. I watch her car pull away and let out a huge sigh as my posture returns to slack, my back and shoulders grateful for the relief. I'm not sure I took in a full breath during the whole conversation. I can smell the chocolate through the container, so for comfort, I pop it open and marvel at the cookies for a moment before diving in. I scarf the first one and stand in cookie nirvana before being brought back down to Earth by my co-workers.

"She's cute. Who was that?" Meghan asks in such a way that I expect her to start chanting K-I-S-S-I-N-G.

I grab another cookie and start munching on it. The rest of the gang funnels into the area after

Meghan. I swallow the bite. "It's not like that. Her name is Kelly. She is the mom of a boy I met last week. She was just thanking me for helping her son." I shove the container toward the other end of the counter. "She made me cookies and they are so good. Go ahead, help yourselves. Way too many for me to eat." All three of them grab one and join me in cookie heaven.

"Whoever she was, she can bake, that's for sure," Carlos says.

"Definitely," Henry adds with a mouthful. "So what's the story, Jackson? You've never mentioned her before."

"That was the first time I ever met her." I stop for a second to think about how much I want to tell these guys and finally decide to spill the beans.

"I went for a walk last week and saw this kid getting picked on at the middle school near my house. I didn't actually do anything, but my decision not to didn't sit well with me, for reasons I don't want to get in to right now." I grab another cookie and motion for everyone to eat up. Somehow, the cookies are making it easier to tell them about last week.

"I missed my stop on the bus Friday, so I ended up getting off near the school, oddly enough, and I saw the kid again getting picked on by three boys, but that time I got involved and scared the bullies off. The cookies are a thank you gift from Coop's mom for helping him."

"Wow, Jackson. That was really nice of you to help that kid out. Way to go," Meghan says.

"Yes. That was extremely nice of you," Henry says with his hand in the container.

"Well ... I felt bad for the kid. He kind of reminded me of ... well, me. No one deserves to be treated like that. He did nothing wrong. Those boys were just being a-holes, taking advantage of someone smaller." I rub the back of my head with my left hand. "I don't know. It just bothered me and I just felt like I had to do something."

"Definitely man. You did the right thing. No doubt. I gotta get back to work," Carlos turns and heads back to the shop.

"Yeah. My list of things to do has not gone down fast enough today. Back to it." I place the lid back on the container and pick it up.

"I'll put these in the break room. Please everybody, have as many as you want." I turn sideways and scoot by Meghan and Henry.

"Thanks for sharing, Jackson," Henry says.

"Yes. Thank you," Meghan adds.

"No problem."

I place the cookies on the table and join Carlos in the shop.

CHAPTER ELEVEN

Carlos told me he noticed a peculiar bounce in my step this week. I was sure I had no idea what he was referring to, but looking back on the last few days, I realize now he was speaking metaphorically and was really talking about my greatly enhanced mood. I still don't think my actions with Coop were anything special. I do acknowledge, however, that my involvement may have helped the kid and I understand the gratitude, but I feel like I acted no differently than anyone else would have in that same situation.

I tend to focus on the fact that initially I failed to help Coop, instead, over-reacting to my own past experiences, and by doing so, allowed a good kid to endure the same torture I once did. My eventual heroic act, if it can be called that, does not, in my opinion, balance my original cowardice. It serves only to remind me of the pain and frustration I hold inside for things I cannot change, for things I wish never happened. They say time heals all wounds. Horseshit! Some wounds, really deep wounds, heal on the surface but leave a rather large scar, a constant reminder of the injury. Granted, the hate and pain are blunt compared to even three or four years ago, but when I dwell for even one second too long on the trauma, I am instantly thrown back to the past, my emotions seemingly only one day removed. What can I do to keep that from happening? Beats me. I feel confident in saying the affliction will always be my partner in life. I want a divorce.

I offer to close up the store so I can wait for Kelly to pick me up. Everyone jumped at the opportunity and bailed at four o'clock sharp. I stay up front and kill time responding to work emails as I watch for Kelly's car. I bring up a browser window and load the website of a local car dealer I see during my bus rides. I've set a goal for late spring or early summer to actually attempt to purchase my first car. I figure by then I should have a few thousand dollars saved up to put down, and my budget arranged in such a way that I can easily afford a small payment.

We had no game nights this week as 1LonelyGurl and ScoobyDont69 needed to be away, mandatory overtime and a much needed vacation, respectively. Instead, I spent my time assessing my monthly expenses. It became clear almost immediately that I piss away a lot of money on absolutely nothing. Just shoring up my frivolous spending and eliminating soda could free up some three hundred dollars a month. That's easily a car payment on something used, and it wouldn't affect my other spending - so in other words, no cutbacks on gaming and movies. I'm sporting a huge smile about that, and deep, deep relief. I will need to eat out a few less times a week and cook more at home, but that shouldn't be a problem.

I don't normally cook much but that is not due to a lack of skill. No one from my foster family could cook worth a damn, so the only way we got to eat anything ... well, truly edible, was for me to learn quickly how to make casseroles and other dishes from combinations of odd ingredients. I became a master of using cheap seasonings and a 70's era brown slow-cooker to make inexpensive cuts of meat more tolerable. I could take some random meat and with a few miscellaneous cans of this or a box of that, make a masterpiece; at least as far as us poor, white trash of the world were concerned. The family sure didn't seem to mind eating good food, and more importantly, not having to do any cooking themselves.

Out of laziness, I suppose, I rarely prepare food at home now. By making my own just two days a week, I will save fifty to sixty dollars a month, minimum. My assessment also revealed how much money I was spending on soda. I didn't just buy 2-liters from the grocery store, which is the cheapest way to buy soda; I purchase at least five 24-ounce bottles from the convenience store or a gas station per week, at roughly two bucks a pop. Do the math. Just cutting the later of those two would equal forty dollars a month. It's easy to see the money stacking up, and with these minor changes, a vehicle and all the related expenses thereof are definitely in my future.

I see Kelly's maroon 2006 4-door Chevy Impala pull into the spot directly opposite the front door, so I quickly close the open programs on the computer and shut it down. I have nothing else left to do except grab the plastic shopping bag containing the sweet rolls I picked up, hit the light switch, and lock the door behind me as I leave.

When I reach the sidewalk, I'm taken aback by the chill in the air, a little early for my taste. This is quite the change from just this morning where I decided to forego my hoodie because I thought it was too warm for a jacket. In October, you never can tell and I won't make that mistake again.

Kelly waves to me. I nod back and walk to the passenger side. When I lift the handle, I find it locked. She realizes it the second I pull the handle out and presses the button when I release. I open the door, get in, and when I do, I catch a glimpse of Coop sitting in the back seat behind his mom. I wave to him. He has his head in a book but has the wherewithal to pull his face out of it for a second and wave back, but two seconds later he is lost again in the written word. I do notice it's a different book than the one that had been thrown in the dirt by the bullies.

"Sorry about that," Kelly says as I sit. The interior of the car is clean. Spotless, actually.

"No problem. Thanks again for picking me up."

"Definitely." I get the feeling she wants to say more as she pauses to concentrate on pulling out of the parking lot, but not another word is spoken by any of us during the three-mile ride to their house.

We pull into the worn gravel driveway of their craftsman's style bungalow. The exterior is aged, red brick with white trim along the roof, doors, and windows. The landscaping is neat but not overdone, mostly perennials and bushes with a few marigolds and petunias lining the edge of the sidewalk. The neighborhood is much the same, with varying styles of mid-century homes, a majority well kept. I feel a certain ... serenity as I look around, like coming home after a long absence. What a beautiful and peaceful place to live. It sure beats my mundane apartment complex.

The cozy living room has older furniture but it's all in good condition. To the right as one enters the front door are a three-cushioned couch and a side chair - a matching pair with faded brown fabric. A black side table rests between them. In place of a coffee table is a bonded leather rectangular ottoman, the kind where the top flips over to reveal a large tray. This piece of furniture is the only other modern thing in the room outside of the television, which snuggles into a large oak entertainment center that was clearly meant for an older CRT television. From what I can tell, they have a twenty-seven inch LCD in the space where an older model forty-inch would have fit. Not exactly a great viewing experience, but then again, I watch way too much TV and especially too many movies, and I suppose others don't put as much importance in that pastime as I do. There is no sense paying good money for a really big television if you just don't give a crap.

Coop still has yet to make eye contact with me and I'm beginning to wonder if I did more harm than good by helping him. Perhaps he's just a bit embarrassed by the whole affair and seeing me is rehashing the memories. Then again, maybe he's just being a typical middle school aged kid going through puberty - always quiet, never comes out of his room, never looks people in the eye, always intensely focused on a handheld game, a book, or his choice of mp3 player. This all sounds oddly familiar.

Coop throws his book bag next to the couch and sits down. He continues reading without a word. I stand near the front door waiting for either of them to say something.

"Just make yourself at home, Jackson," Kelly says, breaking a silence that was starting to make me feel like I was stuck in quicksand with no one around to help. "I'll go start dinner. It'll take about an hour to be done. Here, I'll take those." She reaches out and I hand her the bag of rolls. Before she exits the room, her attention turns to Coop. "Coop baby, would you care to entertain our guest while I prep dinner? Maybe show Jackson your bookcases?"

"I guess," Coop says, despondent. He pulls the bookmark from the back of his book and places it between the pages before setting it down on the coffee table. Kelly disappears through the doorway to the kitchen.

"Bookcases, huh? Sounds intriguing."

"They're in my room. Follow me." Coop walks through the same doorway his mom disappeared through but turns down the hall to the last room on the left. I quickly follow so as not to lose him. The hall is dimly lit with only an amber colored wall sconce.

I step into Coop's room where he is busy making his bed. I can't remember the last time I made my bed. Hell, I can't remember the last time another human being was in my bedroom. Maybe that's a good thing.

On the far wall, I see the bookcases Kelly referred to. The wall is about ten feet across and is completely encapsulated with three bookcases that run floor to ceiling. There may be room for a dozen more books, but otherwise, they are chock-full. The average adult with a collection this big would be impressive, for a twelve-year-old kid, the sheer number is flabbergasting.

I read voraciously as a child but owned maybe ten books. Granted, the foster-fam was poor and we considered ourselves lucky to get a decent birthday present. The best gift I ever received from those idiots was twenty-four hours of silence. When I was Coop's age, I still went to the library, as many kids at my school did, though certainly not as much as previous generations, but that was more a consequence of our station in life rather than the times we lived in. The poorer a child was, the less likely his house would have had a computer at home, let alone internet access, so the library still had value. Regardless, the library rarely bustled with eager patrons back then, I imagine even less now.

Naturally, my experience may have been quite different from the average American during the Clinton years. We didn't have dotcom stock or fancy cell phones. Truth be told, my foster parents never had a cell phone, and the only computer ever brought into the house was an old Packard Bell with Windows 3.1. Don't get me wrong, I thank my lucky stars for that piece of crap. It took less than two weeks for that sucker to break down and the rest of the family to lose interest, and from there it became both my Frankenstein cadaver and my teacher in the world of PC hardware and software. My love of building computers came from those early self-taught days of repairing the ol' clunker.

Compared to even the computers at school, that sucker ran slower than molasses. I often cleaned my room in the time it took for it to boot. That's painful. Whenever I placed a CD in the drive and pushed the button, I had to tap the side panel to get the drive to start running, and even then it took forever to read. Ridiculous. I went through four monitors over a five month period since they kept blitzing out on me. Luckily, there was no shortage of one dollar garage sale rejects available to replace them.

Once I got to high school, I had a giant head start against the learning curve for PC hardware, which impressed Mr. Talbot, my first computer teacher. He took me under his wing and had a significant part in my becoming the uber-nerd I am today. Sadly, he had a massive heart attack two years ago. That was a difficult time for me, second only to when my birth parents died. He was a surrogate parent for me during my teen years. I hung out in his classroom before and after the bell, and even during summer school, if he had class I would often show up just to assist. Now that I think about it, I suppose I was also running from my foster family. Every minute away from them was pure nirvana.

With computers on my mind, I make a mental note of the fact that I have yet to see a computer in this house. I ponder the idea of helping them out with that, but I kick it aside. I don't want to overstep my bounds.

"That's a pretty impressive collection, Coop." I continue perusing but can't quite see enough of the spines to determine what kind of stuff he enjoys. "May I?"

"Sure," Coop says as he finally finishes making his bed. He promptly sits on it, closest to and facing the bookcases.

I walk over to the far wall and scan through the book edges. I have no pre-teens in my life to know what they read these days, but this collection is advanced and full of classics. I see things like *Moby Dick*, *Robinson Crusoe*, no surprises there, but also *Crime and Punishment*, *The Complete Shakespeare*, and *The Time Machine*. I'm in shock. Coop is much smarter than I realized. In this day and age, any twelve-year-old kid who frequently has a book in his hand rather than a Smartphone or IPod or handheld gaming unit is unusual, but also a sure sign of a higher degree of intelligence. A person might learn a little about physics from playing Angry Birds, but wisdom and knowledge are best gained by other means, reading especially.

"Have you read all these?"

"Most. That section in the middle of the far left bookcase is my waiting-to-be-read shelf. You read much?"

I step over to the left and take a look at the place he referred to. "Not as much as I used to. About fifteen books a year, which is a far cry from my high school days. The gaming bug has infected me, so I spend most of my free time doing that. Probably not healthy but it keeps me sane. I will say, you have pretty mature reading taste. Crime and Punishment? A little dark?"

"Good study on human behavior, but I didn't like it as much as I hoped I would. What was the last thing you read?"

"Hmmm ... let me think." I scratch my chin as I try to recall. "Well, I read four books over the summer and haven't read any since. Oh yeah, I remember. That last Stephen King short story collection. That's the one. Awesome, as usual. So what's your favorite book?"

"That's easy. Watership Down. Hazel-Rah. Best protagonist ever."

"Excellent choice. I enjoyed that too." We both stare at the books for a few moments amid silence. I decide to change the conversation. "So, you into gaming at all?"

"Like video games?" Coop asks.

"Yeah. Console or PC or whatever. I play a big online one a few times a week with other people in town. It's pretty fun." I decide to probe a little. "You in to that?"

"Not really. We don't have a computer or an XBOX or anything. I've played a few things at a friend's house where I used to live, but not here."

"Well, if it's okay with your mom, maybe we can play some time?"

"Yeah, that'd be cool. I won't be very good though."

"You gotta start somewhere. I'll teach you everything you need to know." I sense the excitement in my voice at the prospect of having a gaming pupil. I will train this game-boy to become a game-man. Wow. My inner monologue voice just went a little Morgan Freeman-esque. I'm a dork. Recognized.

"You have any friends at school yet?"

"Not really. I've been keeping to myself mostly. Kids think I'm weird, I guess because I'm always reading."

"A little shy perhaps?"

"No, I'm not afraid to get involved or talk to people. It's just when I do," Coop pauses to form the right words. "My mom says I have a way of being too direct with people that can be off-putting. She says people are sensitive and don't always like to hear the truth. I don't know any other way to talk."

"I get that. There is a fine line between telling the truth, yet not hurting other people's feelings when they are not used to hearing it."

There is common ground between us when it comes to our bullying experiences, however, this is one area where we are quite different. Coop is clearly an extrovert that suffers from differences in personality and intellect with the other kids his age, which causes all kinds of problems, whereas I am an introvert that has no problem connecting to people but am often too reserved or uninterested in doing so.

"I don't mean to hurt people's feelings."

"You can't really control that. If people can't accept you for who you are, then they don't deserve to be in your life. There are plenty of people out there who will like you just as you are, you just have yet to find them. But you will. You found me."

"Thanks again for helping me out last week." Coop scoots down on the bed to near the headboard. I join him by sitting on the very corner at the end of the bed, turned part of the way toward him.

"I'm sorry I didn't step in the first time. That was pretty chicken-shit of me. Sorry." I shake my head. "That is one area of this whole bullying thing that needs to change. More adults need to step up and step in when they see that crap going on." I sigh and exhale hard. "I wonder sometimes how many people witnessed me in that situation when I was your age that never helped out. How much less torture would I have endured if someone had?" I rub my face with nervous strokes.

"I'm just glad you did. Those guys got in big trouble at school. They give me the evil eye all the time now but otherwise leave me alone. I wouldn't want to run into them in a dark alley, that's for sure."

"They're just punks whose mommies don't love them enough," I put on a sarcastic frown. We both chuckle. "One thing I've come to realize is that kind of behavior is almost never about the person being bullied, but rather about the person doing the bullying. It's hard to see that when you're young and in the moment. And the later realization sure as hell doesn't make it hurt any less, but it does help you sleep a little better."

As I say the words, it dawns on me that I am counseling myself as much as I am Coop. The pain of my past always seems to simmer just below the surface, always, but knowing what I know now makes a big ol' bucket of water much more accessible when the fire burns too hot. I don't always find the bucket. I don't always remember there is one. My recent near miss with the pills and the alcohol proves that. Lucky for me, incidents like that are rare.

"Boys! Why don't you come in! Dinner is ready!" Kelly shouts from the kitchen.

We both rise from the bed. I wave Coop past me. "I'll follow you in, just show me the way." I flick the light switch off as we exit the room.

The wonderful smell of onion, tomato, and garlic from the meatloaf hits my nose the second I enter the hallway. I inhale deeply and let out an unconscious yummy sound.

"Yeah. Mom's meatloaf is sooo good. Wait 'til you try the mashed potatoes. They're stupid good."

"Can't wait. My stomach is growling." I place my hand on my stomach and I discover the rumble is deep.

We enter the eat-in kitchen. It's small and a little outdated but clean. The cabinets and counter are in an 'L' shape to the left of the doorway, with a square, oak table and four chairs with oval arches and long spindle backs close to the wall as one enters the room.

Kelly places bowls and plates of food on the table as we arrive. There are three place settings with large dinner plates, empty glasses, and folded paper napkins with knife, fork, and spoon on top. All I can think about is how embarrassed I would be if they were to hear my stomach rumble loudly. My abdomen tenses up trying to control the noises.

"If you feel the need to wash your hands, go ahead and use the kitchen sink," Kelly says.

Now I feel like I have to, though I never would at home, because quite frankly, I don't give a rip.

Coop goes right for the sink knowing the optional tone of Kelly's words are meant for me, but to be polite, I follow Coop's lead and wash up before sitting down. He tosses the dish towel my way so I can dry my hands. I fold it in half, then in half again, and place it on the edge of the clean side of the double stainless steel sink.

I take the seat closest to the entrance of the kitchen. Coop sits down across from me. Kelly joins us after filling our glasses.

"I hope water is okay? We don't drink much else around here."

"It's great. Thank you. I drink way too much soda anyways and am trying to lay off. By the way, this all smells wonderful. I'm sooo hungry."

"Well, let's dig in then," Kelly says as she rises from her seat. She grabs the plate of pre-sliced meatloaf and serves each of us two slices. She returns the plate to the table and picks up the bowl of mashed potatoes, plopping generous amounts of the creamy, golden side dish on each of our plates. "Would you care for some Italian-style green beans?" She spoons out some for herself and Coop and waits for my response.

"Sure. Thank you. I don't eat enough greens, unless you count the broccoli from The China Station's stir-fry."

"It counts," Kelly says, though not convincingly.

"I hear the government is calling pizza a vegetable in schools now." I say.

"Well, I think we all know that's a bunch of cockamamie bull crap," Kelly snaps back.

I snicker and laugh at her unexpected response. She smiles wide and sits down to eat. I wait for them to take their first bites before I dig in.

We all begin eating and are too absorbed in yummy goodness to say much. I decide to break the silence in between bites.

"So, Coop tells me you guys moved here not too long ago. From another city?"

"We're from Minneapolis. The doctor I was working for retired and his office closed." Kelly takes a dinner roll from the bowl, tears it in half and starts to spread butter on both sides. "I have some family down here, so that made it easy to choose this area."

"Had you ever lived around here before, and how do you like it?"

"Visited but never lived, and we like it so far. It's certainly smaller, so the pace is a little slower than we're used to, but that can be a good thing. Are you from here or somewhere else?"

"Born and raised."

"You ever think about moving away, just to mix it up?"

"I can't imagine. Too poor. Too scared."

"I see. Well, you're young. Life will throw you curveballs, things change all the time. You never know what the future will bring."

"True. And I know Coop is twelve, but you can't be much older than me, at least you don't look it."

Smooth. I'm sure it sounded corny. She's cute though, probably without even realizing it. When she brushes her hair away from her forehead and tilts her head back, even with that medical office scrub-top on, perhaps even because of it, she is adorable. Then I see Coop sitting there and most of my lust for her disappears like that last tiny bit of water in a puddle drying up on a hot, sunny July day. The mere thought of being Coop's stepdad makes my heart race with panicky, out of rhythm beats. Geez, Jackson, let's not get ahead of ourselves here. You just met these people and you're already walking down the aisle, adopting a kid, and building a white picket fence in the yard. Slow down, tiger.

I swallow hard and look down at my plate to distract myself.

"That's nice of you to say. Well, I'm thirty, but I feel older most of the time." Kelly smiles and takes a bite of the top half of the roll.

"Yeah, I'm twenty-eight, so we're close, but I'm not raising a child all by myself and I have pretty much zero responsibility. I don't even have any pets."

"I would love to get a dog," Coop chimes in. "I really, really want a miniature schnauzer."

"I probably would, except we can't have pets here. Rental," Kelly adds to Coops sentiments.

"In my apartment complex I think we're allowed to but I'm sure there's a hefty non-refundable deposit." I look down at my plate again and realize I have managed to scarf my food down in record time. What a pig. I suppose this could be considered a compliment, to devour someone's cooking, but I have no idea how she will see it. I casually grab a roll and do exactly as Kelly had done a few minutes before. At least this way I'm technically not done eating at a pace twice theirs.

"As you can see, it's just Coop and me. So, what's your family situation? Your parents around here?"

I gulp and crinkle my nose.

"I'm sorry. Is that a touchy subject? You don't have to say anything if you don't feel comfortable."

"No need to apologize. My parents passed away when I was nine."

"Oh. I'm terribly sorry, Jackson. That must've been hard?"

"Yeah, but I was young, and though I do remember them, I just don't feel that sense of closeness I once did. The real problem was my foster family."

"Oh?" Kelly inquires.

Coop continues eating, barely paying attention to the conversation.

"I didn't have any relatives to take care of me when my parents died, so I became a ward of the state. I landed with a foster family that had two real sons not much older than myself, but it was ... let's just say ... not an ideal circumstance."

"I've heard foster care can be really hit or miss. I'm sorry you had to deal with that. It looks like you turned out okay."

I have no desire to continue speaking about them. Please change the subject, I beg internally. I take a big gulp of water then shrug my shoulders.

"Still working on it. I have my moments. It's been tough lately though and I get lonely sometimes. Speaking of, thank you so much for this wonderful dinner, and the company. Best meal I've had in a looong while."

"Glad to do it. Least we could do with you stepping in to help Coop the other day."

"Anything ever happen with those boys at school?" Coop mentioned earlier they got in trouble but he didn't say exactly how. "I don't think they'll bother him again, but it might not hurt to keep an eye on the situation." I kind of feel bad even saying anything. What right do I have to tell Kelly what to do with her son? I'm sure she has her hands full as it is just being a single parent.

"Oooh yes. They got a talking to by the principal. They were told explicitly to leave Coop alone, and if they are seen hassling him again, they will be suspended. They're taking a pretty firm stance, which I'm glad to see." Kelly looks to Coop fondly. "I know he's a little embarrassed by the whole thing, and he's no pushover, but that kind of shit should NOT be tolerated." She looks back to me and smiles. "Pardon my French, but kids like that just tick me off. What did Coop ever do to them?"

"Nothing, I'm sure."

"Mom?" Coop questions, a little flustered by his mom's candid words, and somewhat because all the talk has turned to him and he's sitting right here.

"Sorry, baby. I'll stop." She looks over the table and looks to me. "You all finished? Feel free to eat as much as you want."

"I'm stuffed but thank you."

"Coop, honey, would you mind clearing the table, please?" She rises from her seat and picks up the bowl of potatoes.

"Let me help." I start to get up but Kelly stops me.

"Oh no. You just relax. You're our guest. While we clean up, tell us about your job. What do you do at ACME?"

I settle back down in my chair and think about how to answer. "Well, basically, I'm a big ol' computer nerd. In fact, I'm pretty much a computer god at ACME," I add with obvious sarcasm, but let's face it, it's true. No sense in being coy within my inner monologue. That would just be weird. And I'll just go ahead and say it: I'm a dork. Moving on.

"So what exactly is ACME? Like, specifically, what is the business about?" Kelly asks as she scraps leftover food into plastic containers while Coop plugs the sink and fills it with hot soapy water.

"Essentially, we build and repair computers, mostly for small businesses, but we do a fair amount of work for individuals as well. Whenever a company's computer or an individual's stops working because they got a virus or the hard drive failed, they call us. They bring in the computer and we fix the hardware or re-install software or get rid of the virus. We also have contracts with various businesses to handle all their hardware and software needs, which has turned into about two-thirds of the business. We used to be open just Monday through Friday, but we've recently hired a new guy to help me out and it's been discussed that this will lead to weekend on-call work, just for the business-level customers. Not thrilled about that but I'll deal with it. Money, money, money."

"You may not feel like it, but that's an important job. What doesn't run on computers these days?" Kelly lids all the containers and stacks them neatly in the fridge; a fridge I happen to notice is half empty.

For some reason, I had a created a mental picture of a well-stocked refrigerator, crisper full of fresh fruits and vegetables, cartons of eggs, several gallons of milk, and a door full of all manner of condiments. This is not the case, not at all. The milk and eggs are there, but the drawers are filled with air. From my limited glimpse, I caught things that clearly belong in sack lunches: three kinds of jam, little plastic cups of chocolate or vanilla pudding, red or orange gelatin, pears and peaches. I assume there is a jar of peanut butter and a loaf of bread somewhere in the cupboard.

The organization did suggest a mild case of obsessive-compulsive disorder. Each item is stacked neatly according to item type, all in perfect little rows, and the fridge is the cleanest on the inside I have ever seen. Not a single syrupy ring from a leaky fruit cup, not a spot of spilt milk, not a crumb. In a word - immaculate.

Memo to me: clean my kitchen, thoroughly, before these two ever step foot anywhere near my apartment. Not that my kitchen is dirty, it's not, but Kelly is setting a high standard and I don't want to freak her out and have her running for the door. I'm feeling oddly comfortable around these two, like relatives I grew up with then spent some time apart from, and now we're reuniting. I swallow hard and sigh. It's a good feeling, one I could get used to and it sends chills up my spine and down my arms. I rub my forearms to mat the hair down. I'm happy and I need to stop thinking about this or I might just cry. That would be embarrassing and random.

"Yes, we definitely live in a world full of technology. Might be a problem if we have a major disruption in electricity though. The civilized world would come to a screeching halt, I guarantee you that. Not a pretty scenario."

"Hmmm ... I never really thought about that," Kelly says.

"That would suck. Big time," Coop adds.

"Chaos is what it would be. Children playing outside again, dog and cats living together, mass hysteria."

They both chuckle and I join in.

"I didn't really do a fancy dessert, didn't even think about it, to tell you the truth."

"That's okay. I don't really need it." I grab my belly and give it good shake. "I could stand to lose a few pounds."

"How about we all move to the living room and let's dooo..." She pauses and takes a peek in the fridge. "Chocolate or vanilla pudding cups? How's that."

"Oh yes please. Vanilla for me. Thanks."

"Chocolate here," Coop says as he finishes rinsing the last of the dishes, placing the final one in the strainer.

Kelly grabs two vanillas and a chocolate, and three spoons from the drawer just to the left of the sink. She peels the foil tops off them and places them in the trash. "Shall we?"

I follow her to the living room. Coop is close behind. The light in the room is duller than I prefer and yellow tinged, even with the overhead light and one lamp on, the unnatural and dim setting does not suit me.

My apartment has stark white walls, bright white bulbs of the 100-watt variety, beige carpet, and white aluminum mini-blinds on all the windows. Plain, but vivid and intense. The opposite of how I view my life, expect for the plain part. That fits me to a frickin' T.

"Have a seat," Kelly offers, handing me my pudding cup and a spoon.

I sit down on the end of the couch closest to the front door. I feel as content with that meal as I can recall ever having felt. I could seriously get used to this.

Coop takes a seat on the other end of the couch, his mother takes the chair and sits Indian-style, facing us. Coop digs in first to his dessert, green-lighting it for me. Kelly does the same. We all sit quietly as we scrape the pudding from each spoonful into our mouths. Sweet simplicity. The room holds a serenity and comfort I've never felt around others. I may have, once, when my birthparents were still alive, but not since their deaths. I don't want this day to end.

When he's done, Coop places his spoon and the empty container, licked clean, on the ottoman tray. Kelly does as well, so I take the hint it is okay and do the same.

"Thank you so much," I say. "The pudding hit the spot and dinner was great."

Coop seems restless and uncomfortable, like he's itching to go occupy himself with something else. Can't say I blame him. This whole situation is a little awkward for all of us, so for him, the kid, the one most involved in all this mess, it must feel even worse. I take the hint. We've all had about enough ballooned pleasantries for one night.

"You are very welcome. Thanks for accepting the invite."

"How could I not. Those cookies you brought to the shop made it impossible for me to back out. By the way, my crewmates say thank you. I shared."

"That was nice of you. Would you like to watch some TV or something?"

"Actually, it's been a very long week and if it's okay with you guys, I think I'd rather just head home and get a good night's sleep," Quickly I add, "but we'll definitely have to get together again sometime soon. It was fun." I pray I haven't offended them.

"Oh. Okay," Kelly says as she stands. "Coop, if you just want to stay here, I'll run Jackson home real quick?"

"Sure."

"Just don't answer the door, no matter what."

"Okay, mom. Got it. I know the drill."

"I know you do. Just a reminder." Kelly looks to me and rolls her eyes playfully. "Coop, honey, will you clean up these pudding cups and spoons when we're gone too? Please and thank you."

"Yep. I'm going to my room." Coop stands up, grabs the spoons and plastic containers, and turns to me. "Thanks, Jackson."

I nod twice. "Maybe we'll get together soon and go see a movie or something. Have a good weekend."

"Okay." Coop leaves the room and I don't see him again.

"Shall we?" Kelly snatches her purse, removing the car keys.

I nod and we head out to the car.

On the road, I guide her each step of the way to get to my apartment: a left here, a right at the next light, go straight for a while – all the usual stuff. We don't say much otherwise.

When the car pulls up to the front of my apartment complex, I unbuckle my seatbelt and put my hand on the door handle.

"Sorry about Coop. He can be a little ... curt. When he talks, he speaks highly of you, believe me."

"I get it. That's just the way he talks. I kind of appreciate his bluntness. It's refreshing. At least I'll never have to wonder how he feels. Unlike with some people, you never know where you stand with them."

"I know it gets him in trouble with other kids sometimes. Makes his life harder than it should be."

"He'll be fine. He's strong willed and independent. He shouldn't have to squash his personality to fit in with others."

Kelly nods in agreement.

"Thank you again for the awesome dinner and the ride home. We'll be in touch."

"Thank you. And yes we will. Good night, Jackson."

"Good night."

I exit the vehicle and walk to my front door. Once I unlock it and push it open, I wave to Kelly and she waves back, then she drives away.

I plop down on the sofa, kick off my shoes, and throw my head and torso back to relax. I close my eyes and focus on my chest heaving up and down. A surprising smile forms on my face, a content smile, a smile of revelation.

For the first time in as long as I can recall, the loneliness that often shadows my every step is subsiding, like the sun bursting through a passing cloud. For once, I think my life is on the rarest of rare upswings, and facing tomorrow doesn't seem like such a horrible thing anymore.

CHAPTER TWELVE

My mood on this beautiful Saturday could not be more brilliant. I had a bus ride this morning to a car dealership to check out ... guess what? Cars, duh. I need to start, however, with that bus ride, as it was an adventure all unto itself.

Bus riding tip number four: When the crazy cat lady gets on the bus with a black plastic garbage bag that kind of stinks, don't you dare ask her what she's got there. Don't ... you ... dare.

She sat directly behind me. After a few minutes, the smell became unbearable. Even Charlie started to give me looks in his big overhead mirror, so I turned around to inquire.

"Hey," I said in the sweetest voice I could muster through the stench. "How's it going?"

She was staring down at her lap and muttered something. The only word I could make out was *dead*. That alone should have been enough to freak me out, turn my ass right back around, and continue minding my own business. I'm stupid.

"I see you brought a bag with you. What you got in there? Don't worry, I'm not trying to steal anything from you, I'm just curious."

"Curiosity killed Mitzy, curiosity killed Mitzy. Cats have nine lives, cats have nine lives." She paused from her babbling, untying the bag's loose knot. "Wanna see? Too curious, too curious. Nine down, none to go, nine down, none to go." She pulled open the bag and drew the sides down, releasing a cloud of death.

I peered into the bag and just about threw up in my mouth. My throat actually surged and my cheeks puffed. It was closer than I acknowledged at the time.

I don't know how long the cat had been dead but it appeared stiff, mostly flat, and still ripe.

"Jesus, lady! What the hell is your problem?" I snapped.

She was disgusted by my comment and quickly closed and tied the bag.

"What is it, Jackson?" Charlie asked.

I turned back around. "Dead cat. She brought a freakin' dead cat on the bus."

Charlie did not look pleased at this revelation. I don't think I had ever witnessed a sour face on Charlie. He's just not the kind of guy who gets worked up easily, but I can imagine when he does, the fit will hit the shan.

Twenty seconds later we arrived at the next stop. When the bus came to rest, Charlie slammed it into PARK and forcefully turned the door lever. After unclipping his seatbelt, he burst from his seat, turning to face the cat lady.

He locked eyes with the woman and said, "Ma'am, you need to get off this bus, right now!" He pointed toward the open door.

She mumbled something but didn't move.

"I'm not going to ask you again," Charlie said, raising the intensity of his voice. "Get ... that ... bag ... off of my bus. Move it lady or I'm calling the police. Your choice."

She didn't like her options. In a fit of momentary anger, she vigorously shook her head, her wiry, unkempt hair staying firm in spite of the action. She stopped, grunted, and then decided to obey. She rose from her seat and stormed off the bus like a petulant teenager.

Charlie and I both shook our heads in disbelief. He returned to the driver's seat. Crazy bitch off, doors closed, and away we went.

The car browsing went okay, I guess. I've never been in the market for a vehicle before, but boy did I get some sticker shock. No matter how much money I can manage to save over the next year, a brand new car is almost certainly out of the question, unless I go for one of the subcompact models that can average around sixteen thousand dollars. The problem with them is their size. Being the pudgy bastard I am, I felt like a canned sardine behind the wheel.

So, when the time comes, a larger but used car is probably going to happen for me, which is fine. No complaints here. There was one problem at the dealership though, increasing my future anxiety about the process.

Most of the conversation with the salesman had nothing to do with the features or price or reliability or crash safety of the vehicles I was checking out, but rather with the extraction of information about me personally. It made me feel like I was somehow on trial and I did not enjoy it, not one bit.

What do you do for a living? Will you be trading in a vehicle? What kind of payment are you looking for? How much of a down payment can you come up with? You married? Have kids?

I don't remember the guy giving me a single factoid about the cars themselves. I left the dealership having checked out three new cars and test drove none, the only knowledge gained was that I barely fit in the tiny one, the large SUV seemed like a damn tank, and the pickup truck was nicer on the interior than I imagined it would be. For some reason, I expected the truck to be purely utilitarian, you know, work-truck like, but it was as nicely appointed and as comfortable as any car I have been in. I can envision a nice used truck in my future. Yeah baby, yeah.

After a sort of ... weird morning, Saturday game night is here and I couldn't be more excited. The last few weeks have been tumultuous and electrifying. I could really use some romping through a made-up world, with made-up characters, hopefully in pursuit of a wonderful made-up treasure and skill level increase, with as much made-up blood on our made weapons as possible. I'm not sure what it says about me that my pretend gamer life is far more interesting than my real life. Maybe that's about to change. Time will tell, but for now, the computer is booted, the game loaded, a big-ass box of mini-donuts is ripped open and ready for munching, and the headset is on.

Saturday night online conversation-

RejectGuy99:   Hey peeps! How's everyone doing?

2NE1-KPopper: Doing great. Super duper Saturday fun night is here. Got a B on my Calc mid-term too. Im pumped

1LonelyGurl: Howdy y'all. Goody on you KPop. I guess ur not such a dummy after all

;-)

ScoobyDont69: Hey guys and gal. I hope everyone had a good week. Low key for me

2NE1-KPopper: I get dem grades, I get dem grades, maybe someday I know Ima get paid. – I just wrote that. Skillz. HA!

RejectGuy99:   Easy Tiger! Stay in school. Awesome on the mid-term though

1LonelyGurl: Yeah, KPop – what RG said

:-)

RejectGuy99: Hi Scoob. Week was awesome, actually. Remember that kid I was telling you guys about that was getting picked on?

ScoobyDont69: Yep. What happened?

2NE1-KPopper: Yes. Waz up?

1LonelyGurl: Of course we remember. Do tell

RejectGuy99: Well, Coop's mom baked me cookies and dropped them off to me at work on Monday and asked me over for dinner. So, last night, I went over to their house and she made me dinner to thank me for helping her son

RejectGuy99: It was a nice night and Kelly is really sweet. Coop is really smart too, smarter than me, I would venture. Big reader. Has tons of books. Made me glad I did what I did

ScoobyDont69: Good for you, RG. That was a great thing you did. More people could learn from your example

1LonelyGurl: ^Ditto. Sounds like u made some new friends

2NE1-KPopper: Nice. So, she cute? :-P

1LonelyGurl: What a shock – KPop thinking with his wiener. So ... was she?

:-)

0:-)

ScoobyDont69: Y'all too funny. And LG, you getting jealous?

RejectGuy99: Thanks. And yes, if you must know, she is cute

1LonelyGurl: Hey! Maybe I am. If RG ever agreed for us all to meet, u never know what might happen

;-)

2NE1-KPopper: Seriously u 2, find a pool and dip ur toes in. What the hell u waiting 4. Zombie Apocalypse is coming. Don't wait til it's 2 late

ScoobyDont69: Is Zombies still a thing? When that fad gonna die? But I agree with KPop. Make a date you two

RejectGuy99: *runs away, embarrassed

1LonelyGurl: *grabs RG by the collar and brings him back

RejectGuy99: Ok ok, you knuckleheads. Soon. Maybe we can start with a group meet-up and go from there

ScoobyDont69: That's a start

2NE1-KPopper: Yes. Pizza. Let's do pizza. I WANT PEPPERRONI!!!

1LonelyGurl: Do you eat anything besides pizza, KPop?

2NE1-KPopper: Not really. Me likey. I ate sushi once. Raw fish nasty. Gollum can keep that shit

ScoobyDont69: They have kinds without raw fish ya dope

2NE1-KPopper: *sticks fingers in ear – PIZZA!

RejectGuy99: I like pizza ... or chinese takeout

:-)

RejectGuy99: Anyways, I was thinking about showing Coop the game and teaching him how to play. What do you guys think about him joining our team in a few months when he gets the hang of it? Thoughts, concerns?

ScoobyDont69: I don't see a problem. Show him the ropes and bring him in

2NE1-KPopper: Mos Def. How about his moms? We could use another chick up in this sausagefest. U said she's cute, right?

1LonelyGurl: Do it! It'll be fun havin a noob around to pick on

:-)

Ur a dawg, KPop

RejectGuy99: Awesome! Thanks guys! I'll keep you up to date on his progress. And, KPop, I doubt his mom would be interested. Now let's play!

1LonelyGurl: Let's do it

ScoobyDont69:   Good to go!

2NE1-KPopper: Fine. Y'all killin my sexy-time spirit. But let's hit it. Times a wasting

CHAPTER THIRTEEN

Friday afternoons can be hectic here at ACME. All those promises we make Monday and Tuesday about this project or that project being done by the end of the week are either going to be fulfilled or we're going to be liars. There have been very few occasions where I have failed to meet a deadline given to a customer. Besides, we have excuses we can throw out there that to the average person are too technical to be understood and so difficult to decipher, they stop listening after about fifteen words. They just want their computer fixed, and as quickly as possible.

Luckily, there haven't been any hiccups this week, no lost promises, no overly complicated explanations to give. A small doctor's office, podiatry I believe, needed new computers built with their special hardware installed and software loaded - eight computers in total. Project complete.

When I think about how busy we have been lately, a huge sense of relief lifts from my shoulders knowing we have Carlos around to share the load. Time has flown by too. I guess that always happens when you keep busy. So much so, I've only been able to attend one gaming session in the past few weeks. Luckily, I can do some work remotely so I don't have to spend every waking hour in The Lab, but it keeps me occupied.

One thing I haven't failed to notice during the bustle is the weather changing. The cool mornings of early October have now turned to downright bone chilling while I wait for the bus. I feel bad for the little ones that will soon be hunting door to door for candy. They may very well be wearing parkas over their costumes.

Personally, I've always hated Halloween, but I wish no ill will on those who enjoy it. Children running by, giggling and carrying on, dressed up as their favorite cartoon character or superhero, I can't help but smile when I see it. My memories of the holiday while living with the fosters, however, leaves anger and disgust coursing through my veins. I try hard not to think of it. I focus on the four-year-old girl in the tiara and pink tutu coming to my door - bashful and sweet. I focus on the hyperactive nine-year-old boy donning the werewolf mask, a muffled growl falling flat through the tiny mouth slit. These are adorable things. My own experiences are painful.

The three of us boys would go out, me with the same shitty costume year after year: a stained and tattered white sheet with holes cut for eyes. The fosters brothers inexplicably got new costumes every year from the temporary Halloween shop that set up in the strip mall near our house. They were cheap costumes, but they were new ones and that's all that mattered.

We were each handed a 13-gallon white garbage bag on our way out of the door.

"Hey!" FM shouted, giving the evil eye to both her sons. "Don't act like jackasses out there. And make sure *he* gets back too." She pointed to me as she rolled her eyes at the burden I was.

The older foster brother gave an ill-advised smirk.

With a firm slap to the back of his head, FM corrected him. "Don't sass me, boy, or I'll get your father up out of his chair and you know what he'll do. Now get the hell outta here. Back by eight or you sleep on the porch."

Contrite and embarrassed, the older brother stormed out of the front door, his younger brother right behind. I didn't move immediately. Having been with them only a short time, I couldn't understand the hostility, so I panicked.

"Hey, dummy. Ya going or not?"

I remained frozen.

"Deaf and dumb. Great."

I envisioned receiving a slap to the back of my head too and suddenly my feet reacted. I chased the foster brothers down. They did not wait for me, almost forgetting I was supposed to be with them and the edict of making sure I got home. I didn't alert them to my presence, I simply followed close behind like a ghostly shadow, which I guess made sense considering my costume.

After getting home, the foster parents searched through each bag for razorblades and such, then they collected a candy tax of their own favorites - KitKat and Snickers, if I remember correctly.

Once upstairs we all spilled the contents of our bags onto our beds. Before attending to their own, each of my foster brothers sifted through my stash, taking about half of my candy by the time they were done. I wasn't sure how to react. I simply let it happen. They did replenish my take with all the crap they didn't want: baggies of candy corn, the black and orange wrapped peanut butter taffy, and tootsie pops. Fear kept me from confronting them or telling the foster parents, but I clutched the resentment. I need to think of nicer things.

Physically, despite my past haunting me on a regular basis and leaving me emotionally unstable, I feel better, mostly. There have been a few hiccups here and there pain wise, but I haven't gotten worse. And speaking of illness, I'm not the only one missing the online gameplay as of late. Almost everyone on the team has taken a turn with a cold or an early season run at the flu. Upper respiratory infection seems to be the phrase of the week. Thankfully, nothing too serious, no hospitalizations for my gamer peeps.

It's been almost three weeks since I had dinner with Kelly and Coop. I find myself checking my cellphone every hour just to see if I missed a call or a text message from them. No such luck. I have had no contact of any kind with them, which after two weeks didn't seem like a big deal, but now I'm worried. I was under the impression a bond of sorts had been formed. Maybe I said or did something stupid that I don't realize. I don't know.

The blaring old-fashioned telephone ring of my cellphone jolts me alive and I nearly jump out of my skin. I pull the phone from my right front pants pocket and view the screen. It's Kelly. A strange combination of anxiety and excitement fill my head, my heart races. Cool and kind of weird. I might be a little psychic. I swipe the screen to answer and put the phone to my right ear.

"Hello."

"Hey, Jackson. It's Coop."

"Oh," I answer, a little shocked by the voice. I was expecting to hear Kelly. "Hi, Coop. How's it going?"

"Not bad. I'm sitting in the car waiting for my mom. She ran in the store to get a few things for dinner since we have no food in the house."

"I see. School going okay?"

"Yeah. Things are good. Actually, I'm struggling to figure out what to do for a demonstration speech I have to give just before Thanksgiving break. Any ideas?"

"Hmmm. That brings back memories. Let me think about that for a minute."

"I've been racking my brain and can't come up with anything."

"Well, I'm not sure if this would interest you, but what about a demo on how to build a basic PC? You know, just the hardware."

"I like it ... but," Coop pauses, doubt in his voice. "Sounds complicated. And expensive."

"Lucky for you, you just so happen to be talking to me. Our shop here at ACME is full of old parts, some functioning and some not. I'm sure my boss would give or loan us the necessary stuff, and I'd be happy to pick up the rest, if needed. I got stuff laying around the house too."

"But how hard would it be to do it, but not just that, teach *me* how to do it?"

"It's actually a lot easier than people would realize. I bet over a couple of Saturdays I could teach you enough to get by for the speech. So what do you think?"

"Ummm ... I'm in. I'll just have to talk to my mom about it. I can call you tomorrow and let you know."

"Sounds great." I'm trying hard not to sound too excited but I'm really looking forward to helping Coop out. Maybe he'll take to hardware much like I did.

"You sure it's not too much trouble? I feel like I still owe you for helping me out, and here you are again doing *me* a favor."

"Believe it or not, this *is* actually doing me a favor. I can always use the practice assembling hardware. Plus, teaching someone to do it is even cooler than knowing how to do it. Trust me, it's my absolute pleasure."

"Okay then. I'll give you a call tomorrow."

"Perfect. I'll talk to you then. Thanks for calling."

"Sure. Bye."

"Bye."

I head to The Lab for a hunt.

"What you rooting around for?" Carlos asks.

I pull my head out from between two metal shelves.

"That video card we got by mistake a few months ago. You didn't happen to see it?" I crouch down and rummage through a small box of miscellaneous parts I see on the bottom of the shelf to my right.

"Nope. You sure we didn't use that on the Brinkman job?"

"No, we didn't. I stashed it, just can't remember where. Ah ha! Found it." I jostle loose the card from the box, stand up, and use my foot to slide the box back into place.

"What you need it for?"

"I'm gonna teach Coop to build a PC, non-functioning, for a school project while I simultaneously build him a real one. Henry said I could use a few spare parts from around the shop. I'll have to buy a new motherboard, processor, and RAM, but I figured we had tons of cases and hard drives and junk laying around for the rest."

"You're gonna steal away that kid's youth with that game, you know that, right?" Carlos gives me a smirk and chuckles.

"If I can," I say with a quick double nod.

"Corrupting the youth of America man, one computer at a time."

"That's the way of the world. Won't be long 'fore every damn thing is connected to a computer in some way. Hell, when I was Coop's age, us nerds still got beat up for being into computers. Now nerds are cool. Coop's lucky."

"Some still get their asses whooped for it," Carlos says as he sits in front of his laptop, trying to close up things for the day. He taps a dozen times on the touchpad then types furiously.

"Yeah. It's too bad kids," I pause and think about it for a second, "Hell, adults for that matter, can't learn to embrace the differences between us. Each person on this planet has something unique to bring to the table."

I shake my head as Carlos shrugs. I hit the button on the side of my phone to reveal the lock screen and the time.

"I gotta get outta here. Ten minutes until the 5:20 bus gets here. You okay closing up?"

Carlos pounds the keys for a few more seconds before waving me on. "Yeah, yeah. Get outta here. Don't miss your ride."

"Thanks."

I place a few items into the tote box sitting on the edge of the table, then pick up the box, and head to the break room. I hastily throw on my jacket and rush out of the building, anxious to get home.

CHAPTER FOURTEEN

I had been home for about an hour last night when my phone rang. Coop wasted no time in talking to his mom about the proposal I made, so he called me back right away. I'm sure he was anxious to get the ball rolling. Then again, Kelly made it clear there were a few things that needed to be done before we started, a vetting process, if you will. Even though I had done a so-called amazing thing for Coop by injecting myself into his bullying situation, they still didn't know me, not really, so Kelly insisted on doing two things before she would allow Coop and I to be alone together for long periods of time. Initially, I thought she was being a little paranoid because, well, I know myself, and I'm no meth head or pedophile or anything. After I pondered it more, I quickly realized she was just being a good mom, and that's pretty damn awesome.

Step one in the investigation is a home visit. Because Coop and I will primarily, or perhaps exclusively depending on how it works out, be doing the project from my apartment, Kelly would like to see my place. Apparently, just by seeing where someone lives, a person can ascertain the likelihood that said person is a drug addict, a serial killer, a raging alcoholic, or just a good old-fashioned insane person. I don't fall anywhere on that sliding scale, so I shouldn't have a problem.

Step two in Kelly's government level background check is talking to my boss at ACME. And not on the phone. She insists on having a face to face with Henry. I guess you might call that a personal reference. I don't think I'll have any trouble there either.

All this leads to what I am doing right now, and that is cleaning the hell out of my apartment, and I don't mean that in the literal sense, like hiding all the ritualistic paraphernalia associated with Satan worship. I'm not down with that. I do mean the kind of cleaning that involves actually moving furniture when I vacuum, cleaning out the inside of the fridge, stove, and microwave, and making that bathroom shine, more appropriate for a lady to use than a disgusting bachelor like myself.

Kelly and Coop will be here at noon with a pizza and some breadsticks. Fine by me. By the time I'm done cleaning this place, I'll be frickin' starving. Still on my no soda deal though. I've got bottled water for all of us to drink with lunch - their preference, and mine too.

I open the front door to reveal Kelly standing just in front of Coop. They are both bundled up, Coop with his hands on the edges of a large pizza box that is topped with another smaller one. I can smell the pepperoni and give a little sniff to the air and big smile. I'm starving.

Kelly smiles and pulls Coop to her side. He seems almost embarrassed. I am too, a little. The scrutiny I'm under is somewhat unnerving, but I understand it. My stomach is exhibiting those pre-job interview nerves. Anxious to impress. Hoping I don't say anything stupid.

"Hey guys. Come on in. It's cold out there." I step aside and wave them in.

Kelly urges Coop in first then quickly follows.

I open the tiny entrance closet and offer up its use.

They each take off their coats and hang them. Kelly keeps her purse.

"Should we take off our shoes," Kelly asks as she leans down to begin doing so.

"Oh, no. Not necessary. Dark brown carpet. No worries."

"You sure?"

"Absolutely. As long as they're not dripping in mud, it's no sweat." I look to Coop. "Here, let me take those for ya." He hands over the boxes. "Follow me. We'll eat in the living room where we can sit comfortably."

I turn and walk to the right and place the boxes on the coffee table next to a small stack of paper plates and napkins.

"Go ahead and have a seat anywhere and I'll go grab some bottled waters from the fridge."

I return with the water, placing theirs in front of them on the coffee table. They sat on opposite ends of the couch which leaves me to the recliner. It's not like I'm going to awkwardly squeeze between them, right? I put my water on the table next to my chair.

"I don't know about you guys, but I'm freakin' hun-gry."

"Well, let's dive in then," Kelly says, taking the initiative to pull open the pizza box. She hands us each a plate and we all dive in.

I take a seat in the recliner, and at first, we don't say much as we eat. When most of the food is gone, Coop finally wakes us up with an icebreaker.

"So, you really think you can teach me how to build a computer?"

"Absolutely." I stand up and quickly grab one more piece of pizza and another bread stick, then sit back down. "And trust me, once you know the basic structure, you'll find it much simpler than you might imagine."

"I'm a little worried about the cost," Kelly chimes in. "It can't be cheap for all those computer parts."

"Normally, you'd be right. But like I told Coop, I've got stuff laying around and my boss is allowing me to take some parts from work. Remember too, the thing doesn't have to function, so the parts we use may not even be any good. The point is to understand the basic elements that go into a PC. Any more than that, it would be too complicated and time-consuming for a short demo speech."

"Well, Jackson, it's very nice of you to offer your help. Coop is lucky to have met you."

"It's really no trouble. Believe it or not, this kind of stuff is fun for me. I've been building computers since I was about Coop's age, and as frustrating as it can be, particularly on the software side, the process is rather cathartic. At least for me. Helped me escape..." I ponder carefully how to finish the sentence. A lot of terrible words describing the fosters skitter around my head. No neutral ones come forward so I go with the least offensive one I could grab hold of. "...a bad foster family situation."

"Did you ever know your real parents?" Kelly asks. "And please tell me to shut up if you'd rather not talk about it."

"I did, though it's getting harder and harder to keep straight what is my true memory of them and some idealized version. It's been like, close to twenty years now."

I'm beginning to linger too long on things I'd rather not think about, and I can feel myself clamming up. I don't want to be distant right now. I need to be welcoming and cheerful. I take a deep breath. Time to get the conversation back where it belongs.

"But hey, you guys don't wanna hear about my terrible childhood." I stick out my tongue accompanied by a funny gagging sound. I smile and chuckle.

Kelly nods.

She gets it. I can see in her eyes that her story is full of challenging life battles. Abusive or cheating ex-husband? Both? Who knows? Doesn't really matter, I just know her empathy is real and it puts me at ease. I suddenly remember the reason we're here together.

"So, Coop, I know you're a big reader, but you have any other interests, like sports or anything?"

"I love tennis. I play every chance I get, when the weather allows. You play?"

Coop's eyes are bright with enthusiasm. He holds his emotions so close normally. It's nice to see him outwardly excited about something.

"I like tennis a lot too, however, I've never really played. I love watching it on TV, especially Wimbledon. Something about that grass surface and all the pomp and circumstance. It's cool."

"Yes! Wimbledon is the best. Andy Murray is my fav, though I still like Andy Roddick, even though he's retired now."

"Definitely can't go wrong with Murray. Andre Agassi has always been my favorite player. Of current players, I'd say it's a tie between Murray and Djokovic. Gotta favorite women's player? I like..."

Almost in sync, we both say Azarenka. Then all three of us laugh.

"Well, there you have it then," I say with a shake of my head. It's eerie how much of myself I see in this kid. In some ways, we are so opposite, but in others we are like the same person that grew up in parallel universes.

"I have to say, you have a really nice apartment," Kelly says.

She appears to be at ease, so I think I have passed the first part of the test.

"Thank you. You know, it's a nice place on a budget. I try to keep it respectable. But, I am a bachelor, so I suppose that has its limits." I smile as I tell myself five times to shut up, don't blow it.

"I didn't want to say anything beforehand, but I spoke to your boss this morning on the phone and had a very nice conversation about you."

"Oh yeah," I say with my best version of pleasantly surprised.

"Yep. I will say one thing. He is very fond of you. Spoke of you in a way a proud father might speak about his son."

Part of me wants to cry. I know we have a mutual respect, Henry and I, but I always assumed his oft bleeding heart was for everyone. Maybe with me, there is more there than I ever imagined.

"So," I choke out before coughing to clear my throat. "Did you schedule to meet with him soon?"

"No need. I've heard and seen enough. You and Coop can work on his project as you see fit. I can drop Coop off here next Saturday and maybe one night this week he could come over after school too, depending on what your schedule is like."

"What time do you get out of school, Coop?"

"Two-fifty-five."

"It'd take about ten minutes for you to walk here, so I'd have to take the two-twenty bus to get home by three. I could do that on Wednesday this coming week, no problem. And Saturday afternoon as well." I look to Kelly. "Maybe then you could pick him up between five and six o'clock Wednesday?"

"That sounds fine." Kelly looks to Coop. "What do you think, Coop? Wednesday after school and again on Saturday?"

Coop nods twice and finishes off his water.

"Cool. I'm looking forward to showing you the ropes. Should be fun." I address them both. "And thanks for the lunch. Can I give you guys some money for the pizza?"

"You're welcome." Kelly replies. "And no way. We're still in the red with you. Not to mention this project you're about to help Coop with. So, they'll be more where that comes from."

"Thanks. I appreciate it."

"Well, I think we're going to go ahead and head out. I've got a few errands to run, so, you know," Kelly says as she rises. "Ready, Coop? Anything else you want to ask Jackson?"

He shakes his head. "I'm excited to get started. Thanks for helping me out."

I smile and nod. "Thanks for coming and bringing lunch. I'll see you on Wednesday after school then."

Coop gets up and follows Kelly to the front door. I'm close behind. They put on their coats as I open the door.

We exchange waves after they walk out and I close the door. I remain still, staring at the door. I sigh heavy in relief and feel my shoulders soften, my back slump. I'm not sure why I was so nervous. Worst case scenario, Coop and I didn't get to do the project together. I admit, I would have been disappointed had that been the case. I like the Dansburys.

Now my belly is full and I need a nap.

CHAPTER FIFTEEN

I wave to Charlie as I stumble down the steps of the bus. I nearly end up face-first down on the sidewalk but manage to catch my balance and stay upright. I'm expecting Coop at my apartment at ten minutes after three and my phone says twelve after.

I do my best version of running, which I imagine looks like Usain Bolt gliding seamlessly through the air at the Olympics. I'm sure the reality is closer to a grizzly bear cub falling down a hill.

I get to my front door heaving and laboring to stand up straight. Coop is patiently waiting, sitting on the ground with his nose in a book. We make eye contact. I immediately put my right index finger up to allow myself a few moments to catch my breath. The little shit smiles at my predicament. I can't help but chuckle between my gasps for air.

"You gonna be all right?" Coop asks. He rises, sliding the book into his bag.

"Oh yeah." My heart rate is slowing enough to speak. "Sorry I'm late. Bus running behind."

I take the keys from my pants pocket, find the only silver one, and unlock the door.

"Come on in and make yourself at home. You can go ahead and go to the kitchen. We'll work on the table in there. I gotta hit the bathroom."

"Cool."

After doing my business, getting us a drink, and placing some of the computer parts on the table, others left in the box on the floor, we start the lesson. He takes notes in a green-covered, eighty-page spiral notebook with a blue and silver mechanical pencil.

"So, there are a few basic components to most every PC. It starts with a case." I point to each item on the table as I list them. "Inside that, we install, a motherboard, a power supply, a processor with a heat-sink fan, RAM memory, a video card, a networking card, a hard drive, and a few case fans. Some may also install a disc drive, memory card reader, or other things, but for this project, we'll leave those out." I notice how frantic he is writing, so I stop to give him time to catch up and ask questions.

"Okay, I got it," Coop says, a little nervous but excited to learn.

I take him through installing each piece, elaborate on what they do, then assemble the thing myself so he can get a visual of the process. I figure, everyone learns differently, so just in case he favors actually seeing it done versus just reading about it, I go through the motions.

"So, what do you think? Seem too complicated?"

"It's a lot to take in but I think I can do it."

"Okay. Let's have you do it then."

I take apart everything I did and place the parts back out on the table randomly. Let's see how well he does with one quick lesson.

"Go ahead." I scooch my chair back a few inches, lean back, and cross my arms.

Coop stares intensely at the parts, his eyes darting around, clearly plotting his moves like a good chess player seeing the board deeper than just one turn. With cautious hands and no assistance from me, he assembles the PC like a seasoned nerd.

I inspect his work, peering into the case with false investigative eyes. I watched him do it, I know it's perfect. I lean back again in my chair and give him a few nods and place my hand in the air for a congratulatory high-five. He slaps it with surprising vigor.

"Told you it wasn't hard. Once you know the basics and see it done, no problemo. How about a celebratory powdered mini-donut ... or two or five?"

"Sure. Thanks."

I grab two paper towels from the dispenser and the box of donuts from the counter. I place the donuts on the table between us and flip the lid open, place the paper towels down, bachelor-grade plates I call them, then hand over his water before sitting down.

"Help yourself." I let him take a few donuts before I dive in. We eat and drink for a few minutes, chatting between bites and sips.

"How's the new school going? Probably sucks compared to your old one."

"It's okay. Better now that I don't have to worry about those knuckleheads. Not to be boastful, but most kids at this school seem kinda dumb. I mean, I tend to be the smartest kid in most of my classes. At my other school, I was like ... average."

"I don't doubt that."

"I have a few teachers I like." Coop shrugs. "And the principal seems cool. He really looks out for the little guy, if you know what I mean."

"Changing schools can suck. Other than going to high school, I only changed once and that was when my parents died and I got fostered. Same town, just other side of the tracks."

"I don't know how you did it. If I didn't have my mom, I don't know what I would do. It wouldn't be good."

I feel a brick in my stomach and I'm sure the distress is written all over my face. I miss my parents, more lately than I have in a while. I bite my lower lip and look away for a moment.

"Shit. I'm sorry, Jackson. I didn't mean to," Coop stops, unable to articulate exactly what he believes his words might have done.

I unclench my fists and exhale with a big cheek puff.

"It's alright. It's not your fault. You'd think after almost twenty years it wouldn't still upset me so much. I don't really talk to anybody about it. I've probably been bottling a lot of it up for too long and it's just ready to come out."

"You can talk to me about it, anytime you want."

"Thanks, Coop. That means a lot."

We sit silent, each of us sipping on water. I stress eat three more donuts. I can't remember if I even chewed them. I imagine powdered sugar dusting my upper lip like a cokehead just coming out of the bathroom. Coop resists eating anymore. Smart kid.

I look at my phone. "We got forty-five minutes 'til your mom gets here. Wanna play some video games?"

"Sure."

"Let's head to the living room then."

CHAPTER SIXTEEN

I hear sirens, loud sirens. I open my eyes but I don't know where I am. My vision is foggy and the bits of intense light darting here and there hurts my eyes. There is a voice but I can't understand the words. They are muffled and in super-slow motion. I'm trying to remember what day it is but I can't recall. I do remember being at work. My eyelids grow heavy and I feel myself fading.

Something jostles me awake. Straps pin my arms down so I cannot move them. I feel my body and the gurney I'm attached to slide forward. The temperature drops, so I can tell I'm outside now. The sky is grey with clouds that are ready to rain. It finally dawns on me. I'm at the hospital and being pulled from an ambulance. I don't know how I got here, or why I'm here.

Oh crap. Am I going to die? Please don't let me die. Things have been going well for me lately. I'm just not ready to go. That kind of irony wouldn't be fair at this point. Not for me. Not right now.

It's been six months since Coop and I met. We have formed an incredible bond. I feel kind of responsible for him now, like we're kindred spirits, connected for life, each here to periodically save the other from the horrible shit life will throw our way. I've given him more confidence by helping him realize that his younger years are not the - end all, be all - of his life, and that over time, he will gain more control and buoyancy. And even though I still have yet to take the plunge and meet my online buddies, even with a near constant barrage of pep talks from Coop ... and Kelly, I feel myself getting closer to pulling the trigger on such a meet and greet.

In addition to everything else, I had the absolute best holiday season I can remember. Without any family, I usually spend Christmas alone. I don't bother decorating, and that means no tree, no nothing. I watch *It's A Wonderful Life* and get a little teary at the end, then I watch *Rudolph, The Red-nosed Reindeer* and cheer for the misfit toys to help put me in a better mood.

Henry always asks me over to his house, but I have never once accepted the invite. This year, I felt I had no choice but to spend Christmas with the Dansburys, and it was the best one ever. We had a wonderful dinner, with ham and turkey, dressing and gravy, cherry and pumpkin pie, and the most delicate, buttery homemade rolls I have ever eaten. That doesn't even include the cookies, cookies, and more cookies. After that day, I couldn't tell if my sleepiness was a good old-fashioned food coma or a diabetic one. The next few days left me feeling a little sick, not unlike my earlier mystery illness from autumn. I restricted my food intake and drank a lot of water after that, and it cleared up within the week.

I did take the opportunity to get a computer into the Dansbury home, masked as a Christmas present. Coop took some interest in building them after I helped him get an A- on his demonstration speech, but that non-functioning clunker wouldn't do. Besides, for the gift one, I needed better parts and to build it myself so I could surprise them.

After Thanksgiving, I talked to Henry about using some of the scrap parts laying around the shop, and he was happy to oblige. That, plus some new ones I purchased at cost, I was able to build a decent PC for Coop and Kelly. Naturally, the thing is not as fast and hardcore as my own gaming computers, but it's no slouch either. Coop could use it for school stuff and homework, but I really wanted to get Coop into gaming, and after they opened the gift and realized what they had, I assured Kelly we would keep the game playing under control, more of an occasional hobby than an everyday thing, much like I do, and she agreed to allow it.

Coop was overjoyed about the gift. Kelly was happy but hesitant, giving me a stern look that I completely expected. She pulled me aside a short time later and informed me the gift was too much and too expensive, though she was grateful for the convenience it would allow Coop for his schoolwork. I assured her it was no trouble, and not as costly as it could have been, considering the spare parts and my free labor in the build. She softened up some after that and gave me an extra-long and firm embrace, bringing us both to watery eyes.

In that moment, I saw Kelly in a light I had never viewed her before, not as Coop's mom, and by association, my honorary step-mom, but as an attractive, caring woman, only a few years older than myself. I quickly squashed the idea, one hundred times more fearful than aroused by what it might mean for Coop and I. There are plenty of women out there, and surely the right one for me is hiding somewhere, but there is only one Coop. And our relationship is too special for me to screw up with a poor attempt to woo his mother. Besides, she's way out of my league. I'd have to reach a few levels up to even touch her, and she'd have to lose all sense of her own value to even see me in that light, so I left it alone.

Coop and I, The Nerd Bros, as we've come to call ourselves, have spent the last couple of months just getting his feet wet in the game world, making sure he understands all the commands and the subtleties of the environment. He has taken to it like a champ and is already a valuable member of my gaming team.

As he's gotten more comfortable around me, Coop has pushed hard to get me to read more, and I have accepted the challenge. I went from barely reading one book a month to about three. We have our own two-man book club going too, whereby, we read the same book at least once a month followed by an in-depth discussion about the story, the author, and what we feel we may have gained by reading it. I've enjoyed these conversations immensely. The second book in I quickly discovered how intelligent Coop really is. In a general way, he is much smarter than I am, and it's no wonder he has trouble connecting to other kids his own age, and perhaps, that is why we get along so well.

He's definitely not bashful or as reserved as I am. Emotionally, maybe, but in no other way is he withholding. So, even though we have both been bullied, we attract the negative attention for very different reasons. When spoken to, Coop never lowers the level at which he talks to people, expecting people to have the same capacity as he does to articulate, and this comes off as arrogant, especially to really dumb people who might feel intimidated by his brain. I've gotten used to it, but he sometimes sounds like he is being a smart-ass when he says things. He hasn't discovered that his intelligence is the oddity. He doesn't understand that most people cannot see the world the way he does. It comes so natural to him, and so he assumes everyone must know the things he knows. Most don't, but he'll figure that out.

I snap from my contemplation - a combination of a searing white light from inside the hospital and the escalating intensity of my back pain doing the trick.

"Ahhh!" My eyes and my head feel heavy. We are rushing down a hallway. The beeping and chatter is a blur of sounds. I can't concentrate enough to catch any of the words. My eyelids simply cannot stay open anymore. I feel my eyes roll.

II

CHAPTER SEVENTEEN

Meanwhile...

As he does on most school days after the final bell rings, Coop walks the few blocks to Jackson's apartment to hang out until his mom picks him up. He arrives at the front door and pounds four times. He stands patiently, looking at the ground. Thirty seconds pass. He rings the doorbell and knocks on the door three more times, twice as hard as the first time. Another minute passes and still no response.

"That's weird. He must have got tied up at work," Coop says as he scratches his head. He shrugs his shoulders and turns away from the door. With a little over an hour left before his mom arrives to pick him up, Coop decides to sit on the steps outside the apartment building and read in his U.S. History textbook. With two chapters to read for homework, he takes the opportunity to get that out of the way.

Coop plants himself on the top of the three steps close to the left hand rail, which is black wrought iron with a little rust scattered here and there. He unzips his bag and removes his history book. After flipping to chapter twenty, he quickly skims the chapter to get an idea of what to expect before going back to the beginning to read it more thoroughly. Hoping to see Jackson walking up from the bus stop, he glances up from this book after every couple of pages.

On his eighth glance, Coop spots three people across the street and thinks nothing of them except for disappointment that it's not Jackson. He hears laughter from the other side of the road and looks up again out of curiosity. The face of the tallest one is familiar.

"Oh shit. Please don't see me, please don't see me." Coop puts his head down and brings the history book higher to cover most of his face. The three boys walking by are none other than Nathan, Jacob, and Brett, the bullies Jackson once protected him from. They hadn't exchanged a single word since then, but away from school and with no one around to help, Coop isn't confident they will react kindly to seeing him alone.

The boys continue walking without noticing Coop. They get thirty feet down the way when Jacob, the shortest of the boys, whose blonde hair, long in the front and always falling in his face, turns to watch a sports car pass. Once the car drives by, he and Coop make eye contact. Jacob stops his friends.

"Hey. Isn't that Coop sitting over there?" Jacob asks, pointing across the street. Nathan and Brett look over to find Coop nonchalantly looking to his history book, praying the boys don't come over.

"It sure as hell is," Nathan responds with a mischievous grin.

"What is he doing?" Brett asks.

"Being a fucking nerd, as usual," Nathan says, the wheels in his head turning. "And wouldn't you know it, he's all alone. Let's go over there and see what our *friend* is up to."

Nathan and Jacob hit the curb, eyes darting in both directions for an opportunity to cross the street between the cars buzzing by. Brett does not immediately join them.

"Guys, let's just go. I don't wanna get in trouble at school."

"What are you, some kind of pussy? We're not on school grounds, moron. The school can't do shit to us. So let's go, jackoff, or I'm gonna slap you around after I'm done with him." Nathan adds a fist and a scowl to further emphasize his command.

Brett relents and joins them at the curb.

With only his eyes, Coop looks up again to see the boys hustling across the street, no doubt on their way over to pester him. For months, Coop had enjoyed the bliss of no bullies, no one throwing his novels in the dirt, no one breaking his glasses. He had almost forgotten about his earlier experiences.

When the three boys arrive at the end of the sidewalk leading to the apartment complex, a pit drops in Coop's stomach, his heart rate rises.

Nathan leads the charge up to Coop, Jacob close behind, Brett is not far either but lingers, not really wanting to get involved.

They don't even have to speak. Coop can sense their arrogant presence, their devious aura. With a long, deep breath to help calm down but yearning for Jackson, his mom, or any other adult to arrive, Coop closes his book and places it aside.

Nathan stops three feet from Coop and they exchange a lengthy gaze, no one speaking for twelve full seconds, almost to the point of being awkward.

Not wanting to seem weak, Coop speaks first.

"What do you guys want?" Coop asks with as solid a tone as he can muster, for outward appearance. Inside, he is quivering with fear.

"We were just wondering ... puke ... what little ol' Cooper was doing sitting all alone, so far from home and school?" Nathan's words drip with antagonizing deviance.

"Just working on homework, waiting for my mom to pick me up." Coop points to the building behind him. "My friend Jackson lives right there. You remember him, don't ya?" Coop hopes this will be enough information to keep the boys from doing anything rash.

"Where's he at and why aren't you in there?" Nathan asks, already doubting Coop's words.

"Yeah. Where's he at, douche bag?" Jacob interjects, staying far enough behind Nathan that it's obvious he is using the much larger Nathan as a human shield. Jacob gives up a little more than five inches to Coop, and on his own, would never confront him.

Brett, meanwhile, is looking away, pretending to be preoccupied by something else altogether. He keeps rubbing his forearms and shifting his feet, darting his eyes around and buying time until they can just walk away. Secretly, he likes Coop and wishes they could be friends, wanting no part of Nathan and Jacob's petty harassment. He lacks the courage to do anything about it.

"He's home, but I guess you weren't listening. I said ... I'm waiting for my mom to pick me up," Coop answers in his matter-of-fact way of speaking, often taken for sass.

"You know what I think?" Nathan asks.

"I wouldn't presume," Coop retorts, growing tired of the fifth-degree.

"For such a little punk who's outnumbered three to one, you sure are a smartass." Nathan takes a step forward. Jacob follows suit. Brett stays put. "But anyway. I think," Nathan pauses and cocks his head, "you're here ... all ... by ... yourself." He takes another step forward and is practically right on top of Coop now.

Brett finally starts paying attention as he senses an escalation. He continues to fidget but turns to face the other boys.

"You little bitch. No one here to save your ass this time," Jacob adds, once again talking smack only because he feels safe behind Nathan.

"Guys, let's just get outta here," Brett pleads. "This is boring. His mom is gonna show up and we're gonna get in trouble. My parents will be pissed."

Nathan turns and looks Brett dead in his eyes. "Shut the fuck up!"

Jacob reaches back and slugs Brett in the arm.

Brett rubs the spot, trying to pretend it doesn't hurt as much as it does. He puts his head down, dejected, and takes an unseen half-step back to avoid being hit again, or perhaps to distance himself from what is happening. He wants to run, to hide, but he wants to stay on Nathan's good side just a little bit more.

"Look, guys, I just want to sit here and do my homework until my ride gets here. Why don't you just leave me alone?" Coop plants his left hand down and starts to rise from the step.

Nathan leans forward and plants his hands on Coop's shoulders, pushing him back down. "I think you need to learn some respect you smart-mouth little bitch."

Coop slides his arms between Nathan's and forcibly blocks them away, then jumps to his feet for a more favorable position. There is an obvious size difference between the two boys, in both bulk and stature.

Nathan quickly puts his hands around Coop's neck and squeezes just tight enough to immobilize him, but not so tight that he can't breathe.

"Choke his ass," Jacob eggs on, riled up from his rising adrenaline.

"You listen close," Nathan orders. He pulls his hands upward, bringing Coop onto his tiptoes. "From here on out, you're gonna be our slave and you're gonna do whatever we tell you to do."

"Let ... go ... of," Coop coughs out but is quickly interrupted.

"Shut it, dipshit. I've had just about enough of your mouth," Nathan says, mimicking words he has heard many times from his own father, a domineering and crass man, with no time or patience for his son.

Coop grows weary of the game and the pain from being manhandled, so as the courage to act simmers inside, the time comes to take the advice of his friend Jackson, and stand up for himself.

Most of the time, a little push back, firm and confident, is enough to get bullies to back off. They prey on the fear of their targets, but once they realize they can no longer dominate the way they want, they often give up in search of a weaker victim, Jackson once told Coop.

A fist forms on Coop's right hand, his fingernails digging into the palm. His thumb starts to hurt from the tension, and as his bicep flexes to its max, Coop thrusts his arm forward as hard as he can with a jab right to Nathan's stomach, forcing him to release his choke hold and sending him back three feet, bouncing off Jacob, who is able to stand his ground.

Coop massages his neck and takes a few deep breaths. He stays on his feet, his hands shaking nervously. He looks to the street, desperately hoping to see his mom or Jackson. Whatever happens, he is alone for the moment.

Nathan curls down with a hand to his belly. The three boys don't respond, in shock and not immediately able to grasp the bold move by Coop. When they finally do, Nathan erupts.

"Ooooh! You just signed your death certificate!" Nathan motions for Jacob and Brett. "You two get behind him, make sure he can't run away."

The two boys hesitate, looking to Nathan with confusion. They appear ready to end the confrontation.

Nathan throws up his right arm to direct them again. "Do it! This punk ain't getting away with hitting me. Get behind him!"

This time, they do as they are told. Jacob settles behind Coop on the right, Brett the opposite.

Coop turns his head to each side, noting where the two boys are so as not to be surprised by an attack from behind. He turns back to face Nathan, this time with much less confidence.

"You guys need to just leave me alone. My mom is going to be here any second, and you're all gonna be in big trouble." Coops pauses, then decides to bargain a little. "I swear, if you leave now, I won't say anything to anyone. We'll just let this one slide." Coop swallows hard, desperate for a resolution that will end with his glasses not being broken, or his face either.

"Oh, we're well past that. You fuckin' hit me and I can't let that go." Nathan puts all his fingers together like a puzzle and turns his palms toward Coop, pressing his arms forward to crack the knuckles. There are a series of snaps and pops. He separates his hands and balls up both his fists.

"You choked me, you imbecile. You had it coming. I was just sitting here, minding my own business. You didn't even need to come over here." The words quiver from Coop's lips, though no one else notices.

"Too late for that," Nathan says as he shakes his head, his mind already made up. "Grab his arms."

Jacob seizes Coop's right arm at the elbow. Coop shakes off the contact with a stern look and a sneer right into Jacob's eyes.

Coop glances back to see Brett motionless, and for good measure, he gives him a fist pump and the same sneer as a warning against approaching. Brett takes the hint.

Nathan uses the distraction to act. He puts his head down and charges, releasing a primal scream. His right shoulder collides with Coop's chest and they both fall past the two concrete steps and onto the ground. Jacob and Brett jump back, barely evading the collision.

With the much larger Nathan on top of him, Coop cannot scramble free, though not without a valiant squirming and bucking effort.

Before Coop can even say a word, Nathan sends a brutal right hook to Coop's left cheek, cutting the inside of his mouth, teeth scraping skin. Blood pools in his mouth. Rather than swallow it, Coop turns his head and spits out what he can. Nathan takes it as a further act of defiance.

"Get off him, Nathan. Get off him!" Brett begs.

"Yeah. That's enough," Jacob adds. "He's bleeding, Nathan."

But Nathan is living in his own world, a place where Brett and Jacob don't exist, so he cannot hear their voices. He can hear his own father, Rocco, yelling at him for not taking out the trash, or for being a wise-ass, or sometimes for nothing at all. Maybe his father is just in a bad mood after getting home from work because his boss is a dick and he needs to release some of his mounting frustration.

Life's a bitch and then you die, Rocco would say. After Nathan's mother, Janine, left the often toxic marriage and her son Nathan behind for good, Rocco bore all the responsibility of raising the boy alone, and life for all of them would never be the same.

Rocco spent his days working in the foundry for a small, non-union company, in miserably hot conditions, breathing in soot and chemicals all day. He was forced to tolerate a shop manager who cared little for anything but his own survival within the company and how any action might affect his own workload. Rocco had restrained himself on many occasions from punching that asshole right in the mouth. He had bills to pay and beer to buy, and without a house and drink, he may as well be dead, so he always bit his tongue and went back to work with a fire burning in his belly.

Nathan became an unwilling fire extinguisher early on for his father's inferno. Beyond that, the boy was always lost in the mindset of feeling he was the reason his mother left, which led to his father always being so angry and unhappy. Rocco would never again be able to find anything positive in life.

With his memories of every slap to the side of the head from his father, every crushed empty beer can thrown his way with an order for another, every belittling word about his grades, his attitude, his very existence, Nathan blocked out the rest of the world and saw in Coop a way to release his own anger. He could only endure the abuse and react later, never having been taught how to deal with his anger and frustration in a healthy way, or how to avoid those negative feelings in the first place.

With a balled fist, Nathan holds up his right hand, ready to strike again, but he is drawn from his singular focus by a stern, masculine voice he is unfamiliar with. His eyes, originally locked on the bleeding and helpless face of Coop, rise up to see the man whose voice had broken the spell, though he did not hear the actual words.

The man repeats himself while approaching the boys, and Nathan hears him loud and clear this time. "Hey! Did you hear me? I said, get the hell off him!"

Nathan freezes in place, not sure how to react to the presence of an adult, and still reeling from his anger management failings.

Jacob rushes over, grabs Nathan by the arm, and tries in vain to pull him off Coop. Nathan is simply too big for the much smaller Jacob to even budge. Jacob looks to Brett for assistance with big eyes and hand gestures.

Brett has no interest in his friend's belligerent behavior, so without a word, he turns to the street and bolts, running as fast as his legs can muster, stopping only after getting a full three blocks away.

Jacob stares at the shadow of Brett's presence in disbelief, then turns back to Nathan, giving one last tug on his friend's arm. Nathan leans ever so slightly to his left before the rather large man, six foot-three inches tall with a firm athletic build, maybe twenty years old, reaches the boys and pushes Nathan the rest of the way off Coop.

"Why you messing with this boy?" the man demands. "He's bleeding you little punk." He looks to Coop. "You okay, kid?"

Coop uses his arms to scoot away from Nathan and into a sitting position. He nods in response to the question.

The man turns back to Nathan, and with the flick of his left wrist slaps him in the back of the head. "What the hell's wrong with you?"

"Hey! Don't hit him!" Jacob says, rebellious even in defeat.

"Yo, shut up!" the man snaps. He addresses Coop again. "You know these guys?"

Coop nods.

"Hey, I've seen you around here, haven't I? You know Jackson, right?"

Coop nods again, not really in the mood to vocalize. He finally notices a throb near his lip, flexes his jaw, winces, and places his hand to the area, rubbing the skin with his index and middle fingers to check for blood. Upon investigation, he sees a little. Most of the blood is in his mouth. He turns his head and spits a blood and saliva glop onto the sidewalk.

"Is he home right now?" the man asks. "I'm Greg, by the way. I live right across from him. Jackson fixes my laptop when it breaks. Good dude."

Reluctantly, Coop shakes his head.

"I knew it, you liar," Nathan blurts out. He looks to Jacob. "I knew it." Nathan cringes at the sight of Greg raising a backhand to him.

"Shut the fuck up you little twerp. What are you, some kind of moron?"

Nathan starts to get to his feet, but Greg's firm hand on his shoulder keeps him down.

"You need me to call your parents or something?"

"My mom should be here any minute. Can you just make these guys leave?" Coop feels comfortable enough to stand up. "I don't want them here anymore."

"Sure kid. And what's your name?"

"Coop."

"Sure, Coop." Greg lands a death stare at Jacob and Nathan. "You spazzes need to get the hell outta here 'fore something bad happens to ya. And don't let me see you anywhere near here again. Got it?" He releases his grip on Nathan's shoulder.

Nathan stands up, and both he and Jacob start to walk down the sidewalk in search of Brett.

"Run you little pukes, run! Coop here can't stand the sight of you, so get the hell outta here." They oblige and take off in the direction Brett had raced earlier. "Faster, faster, faster!"

Greg turns his attention back to Coop. "Sorry about those idiots."

"Not your fault. They started messing with me at the beginning of the school year. That's how I met Jackson. He helped me out with those guys, but for some reason, he didn't show up today. We were supposed to hang out after school." Coop turns and spits again, this time it is mostly saliva.

"Maybe he got held up at work?" Greg shrugs his shoulders. "You okay here for a minute while I run and get you a wet cloth so you can clean up a little."

Coop nods. "Thanks."

Greg jogs off.

Coop gathers his stuff and sits back down on the step he had originally started on. He places both hands on the back of his head then draws them forward over his hair until the balls of his hands reach his forehead. He rubs in circular motions, running the events through his mind and hoping the applied pressure will rub out the memories. It doesn't, but the massage helps his headache.

Greg returns with two washcloths, one moistened with hot water, the other gathered around five ice cubes and tied off with a rubber band. He hands them to Coop, who uses the first one to wipe his hands and face clean. He sets it aside and places the makeshift ice pack to the sore side of his face. The chilled cloth provides instant relief and numbing.

"Thank you so much. This is really helping."

"No sweat."

"I just knew it was too good to be true and eventually those guys would try something again."

"Guys like that ain't nothing but a bunch of pussies. If they had to take on someone their own size or one on one, they'd be pissing in their pants."

"I suppose so."

"You need a ride somewhere?"

"Thanks, but no. My mom will be here any minute now, really."

Just as the words escape his mouth, his mom's car rounds the corner and pulls up in front of the building.

The car horn blares. Kelly leans over and peers through the passenger side window and spots Coop sitting on the step with a man she is not familiar with. The rag Coop is holding to his face concerns her. Without even thinking about it, she throws the car into park and jumps out, running straight to her son.

Coop is already on his feet when she gets to him.

"Mom. Don't worry. I'm fine."

"What the hell happened to you?" Kelly reaches for Coop's face and pulls the ice away to reveal a slightly swollen cheek and blood on his lip and the corner of his mouth. Her mouth is agape and remains there for a few seconds.

"I really am fine. I don't even feel it. He chased them off," Coop says, pointing to Greg.

"And who are you?" she asks, grabbing the ice rag from her son's hands. "And where the hell is Jackson?" She pulls the rubber band from the end of the rag and lets the ice drop out. With her left hand, she maneuvers Coop's head to the side and begins dabbing away the blood from his face.

"I'm Greg. I live across from Jackson. I saw some boys messing with Coop, so I came out and scared them off, got your son some ice for his jaw."

"What exactly happened to your jaw, Coop? Who the hell did this to you?"

"I'm fine, really. Greg got me some ice but it's feeling much better now."

"I asked you a question and I want an answer," Kelly barks.

"Remember those boys from earlier in the year, the ones that got in trouble for messing with me? The ones Jackson helped me with?"

"Oh," Kelly says as she shakes her head, rage bubbling up. "That really pisses me off. Why do these kids have to be so mean? Uhh!"

Coop shrugs his shoulders.

"Weren't you supposed to be with Jackson? Where the hell is he?"

"I don't know, mom. I knocked on his door several times. He's probably at work."

"Okay, okay. What's done is done. Let's go." Kelly turns to Greg. "Thank you so much for helping Coop. It is much appreciated."

"No problem. And I'm sure he'll be okay. He's a tough kid."

"Thanks, and yes he is."

Coop grabs his bag from the ground as Kelly places her hand on his back to usher him off. They walk side by side to the car. Coop throws his bag into the backseat before getting in. Kelly waves goodbye to Greg and mouths another thank you.

The drive is quiet. Coop stares out the window, focusing on nothing in particular. The buildings and vehicles and people go by in a blur, much like the last thirty minutes had been for him. He snaps from his trance when he discovers something unusual about the route Kelly is taking. They are not going directly home. In fact, they are on the road that will take them by ACME. Coop's stomach sours. He has no desire for his mom to confront Jackson.

"Where are we going?" Coop asks, knowing full well.

Kelly doesn't answer. She throws on the turn signal and takes the car into the ACME parking lot, pulling straight into the empty space directly in front of the entrance. She slams the car into park, unbuckles her seatbelt, and throws her purse over her shoulder.

"I'll be back in one sec. Just wait here." Kelly opens her door and starts to shift out.

"Mom. Why are we here? It's not Jackson's fault."

She pauses for a moment but the words don't sink in.

"I'll be right back." She exits the vehicle, shuts the car door but doesn't slam it, and heads to the entrance.

She tugs on the handle but the door doesn't budge. She put her hands and face to the glass and peers in. Meghan is standing at the counter, filling out a form.

Meghan shoots a look at the door in response to the rattling. She recognizes Kelly, so she places her pen down and walks over. She turns the lock clockwise and gently pushes the door outward.

"Hi, Kelly," Meghan says with a frown. "You guys on your way to the hospital?"

"Hospital?"

Meghan furrows her brow in confusion then tilts her head to the side. "Didn't Henry call you?"

Kelly's shakes her head. "Why the hospital? What happened?" She pulls her phone from her purse and sees she missed a call from a number she does not recognize.

"Jackson passed out a few hours ago while he was doing something in the back. Henry called an ambulance and Jackson was taken to the emergency room at St. Mary's. Apparently, he has severe kidney failure and is currently on dialysis to keep him alive. He's going to need a transplant."

Kelly places her hand over her mouth, her eyes wide in shock. "Oh no. My god." Her breathing escalates, her chest heaving with each intake of air. "St. Mary's, you said?"

"Yeah. I'm just closing up shop and will be heading over shortly."

"Thank you. We're going now." Kelly waves, turns, and hustles back to the car. She opens the door and climbs in, throwing her purse down between the front seats.

Coop can see the terror on his mom's face. "What happened? What's going on?"

"Jackson is sick and he's at the hospital." Kelly starts the car, fastens her seatbelt, and begins driving away. "We're going there right now."

"Oh my god. Is he okay? What's wrong with him?"

"Kidney failure. Meghan said he may need a transplant." Kelly drives the car in harsh movements with sharp turns, hard braking, and rapid acceleration, her worry for Jackson and the adrenaline forcing her into a nearly involuntary sense of urgency.

"What?" Coop asks with a mix of shock and confusion.

Though Jackson had been sick off and on since shortly before he and Coop met, Jackson did an amazing job of keeping his underlying illness from everyone.

Kelly doesn't respond to her son, instead she just keeps driving in the direction of the hospital, going as fast as she can without getting them killed. There is no need for more words from either of them. The details will come soon enough.

Coop gazes out of the side window as he contemplates the news of his best friend, possibly near death, and a future without his surrogate big brother. He closes his eyes, trying hard to think of absolutely anything else, but the gloom of the situation will not flee easily. Even the harrowing events outside Jackson's apartment that afternoon seem like a memory from another life. A single stream of tears fall from his right eye. He tries to wipe them away but they come faster than he can keep up with.

CHAPTER EIGHTEEN

The parking lot of the hospital is larger than Kelly expects and is jam packed. Rather than drive around for five minutes in search of the best spot, she takes the first open one her eyes catch, three rows from the emergency room entrance and eighteen cars back.

The complex is large and intimidating. From what Kelly and Coop can see, there are at least eight buildings, all connected on their first floors by a series of glass and metal walkways. Two of the buildings toward the rear of the complex are much larger than the rest, the right one fifteen stories, and the left one twenty. All the buildings are a creamed coffee concrete, all the lower corners edged in espresso brown stonework, the many windows are a deep, reflective, bottom of the ocean blue.

Kelly and Coop exit the car and hustle through the parking lot and past the automatic sliding doors. The large waiting room is bright but quiet. The walls are cream in color, the floor is gray carpet speckled in red. There are fewer people sitting and waiting then Kelly expects considering the number of cars in the lot. An elderly couple is on the left, both are reading a magazine. To the right, a man sits with a baby carrier next to him. He is tapping wildly on his phone playing a game.

They walk right past the two sections of seating, straight to the reception desk where a middle-aged woman with her dark chocolate brown hair in a bun is busy typing. She does not acknowledge Kelly right away. After ten seconds, she stops typing and looks up.

"How can I help you?" The woman's friendly tone does nothing to ease Kelly's tension. Her name tag reads Anne.

"Yes, hi. We heard our very close friend Jackson Reed was taken here a few hours ago with kidney problems."

"Let me just check on that for you," Anne says. She turns to her computer and punches in the name – Reed, Jackson. "Here we go. He's been transferred to the ICU. If you take that hall," she points to Kelly's right, "go down to the elevators, up to the fifth floor, and when you come out of the elevators, take a right to the nurse's station. They'll be able to tell you whether he can have visitors or they'll show you to the waiting area. Okay?"

"Down the hall, elevator to the fifth floor, right turn to the nurse's station?" Kelly reiterates, just to make sure she got it squared away in her mind.

"You got it honey." Anne turns back to her computer and resumes her task.

Coop had already shifted to the entrance of the hallway when Kelly turns to walk away. He starts walking and Kelly moves quickly to catch up.

She puts an arm around his shoulder as they walk. "You doing okay?"

He nods.

"If you need to talk to me in private, just say so. Don't bottle it up. This is all very shocking, for me too."

He nods again but says nothing.

They reach the elevator having passed a few nurses, a doctor busy on his cell phone, a member of the janitorial staff pushing a cart full of cleansers and bathroom supplies. Kelly pushes the UP arrow to the right of the three elevator doors. Immediately, the middle door creaks open and they enter. Coop hits the 5 button and three second later, the door slides shut.

Upon exiting to the fifth floor, they find their way to the nurse's station, but before they can engage the woman standing there, Kelly sees Henry about forty feet down the hallway. They make eye contact and each cover half the distance to meet one another.

"Hello, Kelly. Coop. Sorry to see you both under such circumstances," Henry says.

"So, how is he and what the heck happened?" Kelly asks.

Coop stands next to his mom, rubbing his hands together nervously, almost as if he is washing them in slow motion.

"Well, he is stable right now. They have him on dialysis to keep him alive."

"We didn't even know he had any health problems. What happened?"

"Shortly after lunch, he came up front at the store and said he wasn't feeling well. And quite frankly, he didn't look right either. I told him he should just go home and he agreed. He was kind of hunching over, like he couldn't stand up straight, and next thing I know, he turns around to head to the break room and boom – he collapses to the floor. I went down to the floor to help him and yelled to Meghan to call 9-1-1. It was all kind of a blur after that. Next thing you know, he's on the ambulance and I'm driving to the hospital. Crazy."

"I ... I don't know what to say. I think we're just in shock. So his kidneys shut down? Is he diabetic or something?" Kelly rubs the back of her head and neck, puzzling over the idea.

"They say he has PKD, ummm, polycystic kidney disease. It's hereditary and there is no cure. He's going to need a kidney transplant, and soon."

"Can we go see him?" Coop finally chimes in.

"I'm sure you can, but ... he's been in a sort of comatose state for a while now," Henry answers, placing his hand on Coop's shoulder to comfort him. "How you handling all this? I know you guys were like best buds."

"Brothers," Coop corrects.

Henry understands and nods to acknowledge it.

"Well, he's obviously pretty high up on the transplant list, so that's good, but he's A B negative, which will make it harder to find a suitable donor."

"What about family? Certainly he has someone around here. What about his foster family? I assume they have been notified?" Kelly asks.

"They have not and there has been some debate about it. Anyone who knows Jackson understands he has no contact with them, and it's not like they adopted him or anything, so from a legal standpoint, they're not technically family. He has no other real family that anyone knows of."

"That's a shame. And yes, we know all about his foster family. I just thought, considering the situation," Kelly wobbles her head with indecision then shrugs her shoulders.

"Absolutely not!" Coop barks.

"Coop? What?" Kelly asks.

"He would kill all of us if you called them. They cannot come, no ... matter ... what. Jackson would not want them here, period. Trust me on this one. He's told me things ... things he's never told anyone, and believe me, bringing them here would be devastating and a big, big mistake. DO NOT!"

Kelly and Henry exchange a look of concurrence.

"Okay, Coop. I think we can understand that," Kelly says. She turns her attention back to Henry. "You know what really worries me?"

"What's that?"

"No insurance. How the hell is he going to pay for all this?"

Henry shakes his head. "I've heard these kinds of things can run a hundred grand. And that doesn't include the after care. I'm definitely worried about that too."

"I take it he made no effort to sign up for healthcare this year?" Kelly asks.

"Nope. He has a strong aversion to doctors for whatever reason, money wise I would guess, so he opted to just pay the fine this year instead of getting coverage. This is a perfect example of why the healthcare bill needed to happen. A young guy like Jackson gets seriously ill and doesn't have insurance. So what happens? They'll save his life, no question about that, but then what? The hospital's a not-for-profit, they may cover some of it, but as things mount, Jackson will likely have to file bankruptcy to get out from under the bills. We all end up paying for it one way or another."

Coop is stoic, taking in all the information while the gears in his head grind and spin. The embers of a growing fire emerge. He keeps all his thoughts inside though, letting them twirl around like a feather in the wind he can't quite grab.

"You guys should go in and see him. Follow me." Henry turns and walks back the way he had come from. When they reach the fifth door down on the left, Henry puts his arm out to allow Kelly and Coop to enter. "I'll wait out here."

The room smells of disinfectant and is quiet except for the faint beep of the heart monitor. A 22-inch television is mounted to the wall opposite the bed, just above and to the right of a large dry erase board with nothing written on it. Two vinyl-covered recliners are in the corner directly across from the door.

Kelly steps to the right edge of the hospital bed and looks to Jackson with trepidation. She gently places her right hand on his blanket-covered foot and weeps.

"Oh, Jackson," she says through the sobbing. The dozens of tubes and wires coming and going from the different parts of Jackson's body do nothing to quell her fears.

Coop stops at the corner of the wall but cannot drive himself to enter further. He just stares at the end of the bed, fixated on the chart dangling there. His eyes dart up but back down again. What he sees in the blur is not his best friend Jackson but something that reminds him more of Darth Vader without the black mask – a pale face, tubes across his face and into his nose, a sickly shell of his former self.

Kelly turns to see her son standing aloof. "Come over here honey. I know it's a little unpleasant, but this is Jackson laying here, your big bro, and he needs to feel your presence. Come."

With loathing in his eyes, Coop turns and steps forward. Kelly shifts to the left to allow him past. He settles near the middle of the bed and finally looks to Jackson's face for longer than a glimpse. Kelly rubs Coop's lower back to comfort him.

"Is he going to be okay?"

"I don't know baby," she answers, shaking her head. "I sure hope so."

A woman in soft pink scrubs, five and half feet tall with a stocky build walks in with determination. She keeps her dishwater blonde hair in a bun on the top of her head, preventing it from getting in her face when she leans over her patients and their beds. The badge clipped to her scrub top has a picture of her from two years ago when she first started working in the intensive care unit, and her name – Courtney Jensen, R.N.

"Hi ya'll," Nurse Jensen announces. "If it's okay, can I just squeeze in there? I'll be real quick and then get out of your way. Gotta make sure everything is still flowing." She smiles wide with the kind of smile that just shatters the sour mood of any room she enters; a wonderful attribute to have in the midst of such a serious environment.

The word that pops into Kelly's head when she turns to see the nurse is sunshine. Her own emotional state softens in Courtney's presence. She steps to the other end of the bed to make way.

Coop turns but doesn't make eye contact with the nurse, instead choosing to move to one of the recliners so he can sit back and watch, offering himself some distance physically, if not psychologically, from the situation.

"How do you two know Jackson? Pretty serious stuff here but we're gonna take real good care of him." Nurse Jensen busies herself checking all the connections from the various tubes and wires, pressing buttons on the monitor, and adjusting the pillow behind Jackson's head.

"Well ... uh, we're very, very good friends of his, practically family," Kelly answers. "He and my son, Coop here, are like brothers."

"That's nice. I'm glad he has someone here that cares about him. He'll need people here to help him get through this. It won't be easy."

"So what's the full story here? Henry mentioned PKD when we got here. What can be done? And please don't sugarcoat it."

Coop sits silent but listening intently.

"The PKD basically causes tumors to form on the kidneys, rendering them useless. To make matters worse, he had other underlying issues that I can't really discuss in detail. It was all a perfect storm really, but even under ideal conditions, the PKD would likely have surfaced at some point. Just a short time ago, he was put on the transplant list. We can keep him going for a while, but ... not forever." For the first time since she had entered the room, Courtney's smile turns to a frown. "We'll do our very best, I promise you that. I'm really sorry."

"What are the chances of him finding a suitable match for transplant?" Kelly continues to question.

Nurse Jensen finishes her check of Jackson and stays by his side. "It's really hard to say. The availability is tricky and changes all the time. He's otherwise pretty healthy and at his age, he's a good candidate. We'll keep our fingers crossed."

"This is all just ... so shocking. No one had any idea he was even sick." Kelly places her hand over her mouth, closes her eyes, and tries hard to keep from crying again. She holds back, for the moment.

"Well, being of the ultra-stubborn male of our species, he may have had symptoms for some time and just managed to keep them a secret honey. Men are scared of going to the doctor, we all know that. Even to their own detriment."

"Can he hear us?" Coop springs out of nowhere.

Kelly and Courtney lock eyes, and without saying a word, ask each other how best to answer that question. Kelly shrugs her shoulders.

"I like to believe he can," Courtney answers. "If you have something you need to say him, I would do it soon. You don't wanna have any regrets. I do have to run, but I'll be back later, off to save more lives." She smiles wide and leaves the room with quick steps.

Coop jumps from his seat. "Mom, I need to be alone for a few minutes." He doesn't even look at her, just walks over to Jackson's bedside and waits.

Kelly just nods and starts to walk out of the room but stops just short of leaving. "I'll be right out here talking to Henry. Take your time baby. I love you." She opens the door and exits, shutting it behind her.

Next to his friend, Coop stands quiet, his left hand on his own chest, the other in his pocket, glaring at the area around Jackson's hip.

The only motion and sound in the room is the whoosh and beep of the dialysis machine and the other health monitors. For Coop, the entire rest of the world does not exist in this moment - there is only he and Jackson, alone in a confusing world full of brick walls, racing hearts, and hopeful sorrow. Coop struggles to grasp the tangled emotions, the numbness of having a life hanging in the balance with no power to act, and no rationale from unknown gods about the unforgiving nature of life and death.

He closes his eyes, takes in a deep breath, then as he releases the air from his lungs in a calm, paced manner, he opens his eyes and lifts his head to see his friend's face.

The clear, plastic oxygen mask over Jackson's face is the most prominent feature, and the most disturbing, though Coop's not sure why. The severity of his friend's condition is even more evident by the mild jaundice and the gentle heaving of Jackson's entire upper body in time with the pumping of the machines, the crisp, white sheet pulled all the way up to Jackson's shoulders moving the same. Coop cannot help but recall the day's earlier trouble with Nathan, Jacob, and Brett, and it brings to light how special his relationship to Jackson really is. Coop wishes to turn back the clock to a time when he had not just been attacked by Nathan, and a time when his friend was not sick.

As his eyes water, Coop looks away for a moment, using all the power he has not to break down and cry. Staring into the corner of the room, he takes in and releases a dozen deep breaths, calming himself enough to continue.

Mustering bravery he isn't certain he has, Coop puts his left hand into Jackson's left hand and returns his eyes to the quiet and still face of his friend.

"I don't know if you can actually hear me or if that nurse is just full of crap, but I have a few things I need to say to you, just in case you," he stumbles for the right words and swallows hard, "in case you don't make it.

"Oh crap, we're guys. We don't get all sappy and lovey-dovey with each other. Right? I guess under the circumstances and just in case this is the last time we speak, it's probably okay.

"I just don't know how to say what I really need to, things I've always wanted you to know but just couldn't.

"How do I thank you for saving me from those idiots at school and for showing me how to stand up for myself?

"How do I tell you that having a friend like you ... has made me more confident and less scared, in everything I do?"

Coop's tone quickly changes from grateful to contrite upon remembering a conversation he and Jackson had a few months back. He remembers calling Jackson a big pussy for never meeting up in person with his gaming team, especially 1LonelyGurl, since he clearly has a major crush on her and is dying to ask her out on a proper date. Jackson was offended at the time but got over it fast and never thought about it again. Thinking about it later, Coop eventually understood how his poor choice of words, even said in jest, were hurtful to his friend, and how it made Jackson feel inferior because of his shy nature and introverted personality. It mirrored Coop's situation in how he is always left feeling like an outcast for being too direct. Coop never got around to apologizing for his words that day, but he dwelled on it. He only wished Jackson was awake and alert, and could hear him now.

"I'm sorry if I'm a little too direct sometimes. I don't mean to be. I hope you understand that I've never said anything with the intent of hurting you. I know my personality challenges you at times, and honestly, you do the same to me. When I say too much, you don't say enough. I hope we are both better people for having known one another. I know I am."

Coop looks to the ceiling with a heavy sigh. He takes in and releases two deep breaths then looks back to his Jackson. His eyes instantly well up.

"Damn it, Jackson!" He closes his eyes, tears escaping the corners of his eyes and streaming down both cheeks.

Sobbing, Coop opens his eyes again. He squeezes Jackson's hand, twice as hard as he started with. "You need to get better. You cannot die on me. Not now, not ever. I..."

Coop loses his train of thought and jumps onto another track, one that floods his mind with ideas flying by so fast he can barely retain them.

He releases his grip and rubs the sides of his head with both hands.

"I need to go. I'm going to help you, Jackson. Just hang on. Hang on for me."

He spins around and rushes from the room, meeting his mom, Henry, and Meghan in the hallway.

"How you doing, Coop?" Kelly asks sympathetically.

Coop nods twice. "I need to get tested, right now." There is no manner of compromise or discussion to be had in his voice.

Kelly understands exactly what he means but the protective mother in her internally rebuffs the idea. She tries hard to keep her feelings from erupting on her face but she fails. Coop sees them instantly.

"Damn it mom! I'm doing this."

"Cooper Dansbury! Mouth!"

"What mom? I can't just sit by and watch him die if there is any chance whatsoever that I can do something to help him. I'm forming a plan. The first part is finding out whether or not we are compatible so I can donate a kidney. That's number one. The other parts I'm still mulling around with and I'll work out tonight, but right now, you need to let me do the right thing."

Henry and Meghan look to each other in disbelief and work hard to not make eye contact with Kelly or Coop.

"Mother?"

Kelly takes a deep breath and knows what she must do, despite her fear, her doubt.

"Okay, Coop. I'll tell you what, I'll get tested too. How's that?"

"Thank you, mom."

"You know what?" Henry intercedes. "I'm going to get tested too."

"Definitely. Me too," Meghan adds. "I'm healthy and he needs our help, so I'm in."

Coop is overjoyed that everyone is following suit. He smiles wide causing pain to his injured lip and jaw, a reminder of his earlier encounter. He rubs the area with his left hand but brushes off the pain and the negative thoughts just as quickly as they had arrived.

"Stay here with Henry. I'll go talk to a nurse about all of us getting tested." Kelly turns and walks to the nurse's station.

"Everything is going to be fine," Henry says in an attempt to keep spirits high.

Coop stares off into space, his master plan to save Jackson rolling through his mind like wave after wave crashing to the beach during a storm.

"I just know he's going to pull through," Meghan says.

Out of the corner of his eye, Coop spots the blurry figure of a woman coming closer. His mom arrives back at the group.

"Hey guys. The charge nurse says they will test us all right now if we are willing," Kelly says as she rubs Coop's back.

"Well, we might as well since we're all here and time is a wasting for our friend," Henry says.

"Perfect," Coop says. "I'll go first."

"Oh, by the way, I asked what the cost was for doing this blood work would be. It's kind of steep. One hundred five dollars each."

"Ouch," Meghan says with a frown.

"Don't worry about it," Henry responds. "I'll take care of that for the four of us. The least I can do."

"Are you sure, Henry?" Kelly asks. "That's a lot of money."

"Worth it. There's only one Jackson and I'll do whatever I can to help out. This is just one small way I can do that."

"Let's do it then," Meghan says.

"Okay. I'll let the nurse know we are good to go." Kelly walks back to the nurse's station and shares that the four of them are ready to be tested.

One by one, they take turns getting blood drawn to be tested for blood type, antigen match, and cross match. Beyond that, if one or more donor candidates is found, medical histories psychological evaluations, and in-depth physical examinations will still need to be performed to make sure the donor is in proper health and capable of completing the act.

"The nurse said the results will be available tomorrow, late in the day," Kelly says, the four of them standing near the nurse's station. "If anyone is a match, there will be additional health screenings necessary before actually donating, but we can deal with that should the time come. I have to work tomorrow and Coop has school, so we really need to head home, pick up some dinner."

"Yeah," Henry agrees. "It's been a long day for everyone."

"We'll come back tomorrow after work and check in on him. Hopefully we'll have the results by then so we know where we stand with that." Kelly places her hand on Coop's back.

"I'll come by too," Henry adds. "There's not much more any of us can do until then anyway. You guys have a good night and we'll talk tomorrow one way or another.

"Good, let's go. I've got a lot to do," Coop cuts in.

"We'll see you guys tomorrow then," Meghan says. She offers a hug to Kelly, who gladly accepts. "Have a good night." She hugs Coop as well.

"Thanks. You do the same," Kelly says. She and Coop head down the hall toward the elevators. The adrenaline has worn off and they are both growing weary.

Meghan stands by as Henry takes the paperwork offered to him. The charge nurse instructs them on where to take it to settle the payment for services.

"So, I guess I'll see you at work tomorrow." Meghan says.

"Yep. You have a good night and we'll see you in the morning."

They walk down together, splitting off when they reach the finance office.

Meghan heads out to her car and drives straight home.

Henry takes care of the bill and goes home as well.

CHAPTER NINTEEN

Coop flies through the front door, his mission clear, his mind of singular focus. He stops in the hallway for a split second trying to decide where he will work for the evening, finally choosing the kitchen. He walks that way and tosses his backpack on the table, then spins right back around and hustles to his room in search of supplies.

From the top drawer in his dresser he removes a fresh spiral notebook - seventy pages and college ruled. Back in the kitchen, he sits at the table to begin crafting his master plan. From the zippered front pouch on his backpack, he chooses his favorite kind of pencil, a standard yellow #2, and flips to the first blank page of the notebook.

Kelly tosses her purse on the couch and takes the fast food bag to the kitchen trash can.

"You need any help?"

"No, mom." Coop scribbles furiously, flipping from page to page as he fills the lines with his master plan, one he hopes will help save his friend.

"Well, I'm going to watch a little TV before bed. If you need anything, let me know." She steps over to her son and plants a kiss on the top of his head. "I love you honey." She leaves the room, ready to sit and relax after a long, emotional day.

Coop is already too distracted to acknowledge his mom. He has a plan to help Jackson, and time is not on his side. To accomplish his plan, many things would have to fall into place. He holds some concern that not everyone will back his ideas or that the logistics will be too cumbersome, but rather than focus on the impossibilities, he puts all his energy into believing it will work, despite his anxiety. The life of his best friend is at stake, so his determination holds firm.

Ninety minutes pass and Kelly is ready to call it a night. She turns off the TV, checks to make sure the front door is locked, and turns off the living room light. She goes to the kitchen to check on Coop.

"So, you haven't said much about what you're up to. Can I give it a look?"

Coop shields the page from his mom. "No. I'm not ready yet. I'll let you see it when it's done."

"And when do you think that will be? It's getting late."

"I need just a little more time."

"Well, I'm going to bed ... and you have thirty more minutes, so finish up or it'll have to wait until tomorrow. I know it's been a rough day and we've got a lot to process." She bends over and kisses Coop on the cheek. She knows her son and can see how involved he is, so she doesn't press too hard. "Good night. Thirty more minutes."

She stands behind her son for a few moments, staring at his reddish-brown wavy hair, worrying about his psyche, melancholy herself. She's never had to counsel Coop in this way, and she doesn't feel the least bit equipped to do so. She goes to bed with her body exhausted, her mind turning.

CHAPTER TWENTY

Kelly wakes up before Coop, as she always does, takes a shower, and gets dressed. With only one bathroom in the house, her routine keeps the bathroom battles to a minimum, not that Coop requires much time in there.

At 6:45, she pokes her head into Coop's room to discover he is already out of bed. She shrugs her shoulders but still finds it odd. She can't remember the last time her son was up and out of bed before her wake up nudge. He sleeps like a rock and has always had trouble rising before seven o'clock. Kelly usually makes an attempt every five minutes until he gets annoyed enough to crawl out of bed and make his way to the bathroom. Even though this is a rare occasion, Kelly understands why he might not have slept well.

Kelly walks to the kitchen and stops short of entering when she sees Coop at the table, hunched over and fast asleep, his left cheek pressing against the open spiral notebook he had so furiously filled with information. He is still wearing the clothes he had on the night before. It dawns on Kelly that Coop never made it into bed. She smiles, proud of her son's commitment.

With gentle steps, Kelly moves next to her son. After a few blissful moments of just watching him sleep, she carefully brushes the hair from his eye. It mostly falls back in place and his face comes to life with a twitch of his cheek.

In a whisper, "Coop, honey, it's time to wake up."

Coop snaps from his trance and lifts his head. The pencil he was writing with is stuck to his cheek.

Kelly belly laughs at the ridiculous sight of the yellow #2 pencil hanging from temple to chin on her son.

Coop looks to his mom and still groggy says, "What?" He scratches an itch on his forearm but is still unaware.

"Ummm ... you have a," she pauses and makes circular motions in the air with her index finger in the general direction of his face, "a little something on your face." She puts her hand over her mouth and laughs some more.

"Where?" He brushes his nose trying to discover what Kelly is referring to.

She busts out laughing again.

Coop finally discovers the pencil by patting his cheek. He slowly peels the painted wood away from his skin and he can't help but join his mother in a chuckle.

"Why don't you go take a quick shower to get woken up and I'll make pancakes for breakfast."

"Okay." Coop stands up and pushes his chair back under the table. He returns the pencil to his backpack and is closing the notebook when Kelly interrupts.

"Can I see what you've been working so hard on? Maybe I can help."

He holds the spiral in his hand and just stares at it for a moment. He flips to the final pages, proofreading them fast to remind himself of the last things he worked out before dozing off. After pondering for a few more moments, he places the notebook back down on the table and places his hand on it, like he's having a hard time letting go of it.

"Okay," Coop finally answers. "But I don't think I need any help. I think I got it all covered." He starts to walk out of the kitchen then turns abruptly. "And don't worry about the pancakes, cereal will be fine. I would like to leave a little early today. I need to talk to Principal Owen before school starts."

"Okay. We can do that."

"Thanks." Coop continues on to get his shower.

Before sitting down, Kelly grabs a bowl from the cabinet, a spoon from the utensil drawer and places them on the table alongside a box of Cocoa Krispies.

She sits in the seat to the left of where Coop slept and picks up the notebook, happy to finally be able to satisfy the curiosity of her son's unknown whim. She reads intently until reaching the end of the pages. Upon closing the cover of the notebook, Kelly puts her right hand over her mouth and breaks down into soft tears, and not tears of sadness, but of pride and delectation for her son and his brilliance. In this moment, she has never been more proud of her son, more in awe, and more in love with him.

Coop emerges from the hallway with his bathrobe on to find his mother crying. Finding her in such a state frightens him. His first thought is that some bad news had come through about Jackson.

"Mom? What's going on?" His voice is loaded with worry.

Kelly sniffs hard and wipes the tears from her face with both hands before turning to answer Coop. "Oh, Coop. This ... this ... is so wonderful. I don't know what to say. Jackson is lucky to have such a caring and thoughtful friend."

The stress in Coop's body releases. "Geez, you scared the crap out of me."

"I'm sorry. Oh honey. This is a great plan, so thorough. And I tell you what. We're going to do everything in our power to make this happen and we won't quit until we do. I'm very proud of you. We'll need to get you to school a little early, so good choice on the cereal. It'll save a ton of time."

"Yep. And I'll take care of it so you can get ready for work." Coop turns and starts walking back down the hallway. As he walks, he yells back, "I'm going to get dressed real quick first."

Kelly gets up from the table and goes to her bedroom to finish getting ready.

CHAPTER TWENTY-ONE

For the third time since the start of the school year, Coop steps through Principal Marcus Owen's office door. The first was with his mother when he registered as a new student just before the school year began. Coop's initial impressions of Principal Owen were all positive. He was young, friendly, approachable, yet serious about education and the future of his students.

Marcus started out as a history teacher within the school district upon getting his teaching certification, but the journey had only just begun for him. He never stopped taking night classes after securing a job at Jefferson High. During the day he taught U.S. History to sophomores and at night he worked diligently on his Master's, eventually going as far as a Doctorate in Education.

Just before his thirtieth birthday, Marcus heard a middle school in the district had a principal retiring, so he applied and lobbied the appropriate higher-ups, and his never quit attitude made him the youngest ever principal in District 78. Still young and full of spunk, he connected to the teachers and students in a way no one could see coming. The school rallied behind him to improve test scores and create an environment that made teachers happy to come to work, and more importantly, made students eager to learn. He was a disciplinarian, but only when he had to be and only when it served to motivate. Most of the time, he used a perfect blend of facts, examples of harsh reality, and a genuine caring for those in his tutelage to keep everyone on task and on his side. When he told a person how much he cared about their circumstance, their life, their future, they knew he meant it. In doing so, teachers and students alike learned to care more about their own welfare knowing they had someone of power in their corner that would put in the work, show up at their house when times got tough, and put plans into action without fear, without doubt.

The second time Coop and Principal Owen met in that office was after the bullying incident involving Nathan, Jacob, and Brett, the same one Jackson saw fit to inject himself. Principal Owen threw down the gauntlet on those boys, going just short of suspending them. He only handed down out-of-school suspensions in the most extreme cases, and though he considered their behavior horrible, he believed the boys would be better served under his intense scrutiny as opposed to doing god-knows-what at home. They received detention for two straight weeks and they had to clean the boy's locker room, twice, top to bottom. They also got some sensitivity lessons from the school psychologist, Dr. Margarite Swenson.

"Hello, Coop. Take a seat." Principal Owen remains in his executive, burgundy leather office chair, motioning to the chairs in front of his desk.

With his backpack in hand, Coop takes a seat in the right-hand chair in front of the desk. He unzips the backpack and removes the notebook he had written down his plan of action, flipping to the first page and folding the cover behind.

"So, what can I do for you today?" Principal Owen points to his own face in reference to Coop's. "Everything okay?" he asks.

"Not really."

"Oh?"

"Well, I'm fine, but my friend Jackson is really sick and is going to need a kidney transplant or he will probably die." Coop had already decided not to mention his recent incident with Nathan, Jacob, and Brett. He didn't want to muddle his request, taking focus from the more pressing issue. The time would come, however, for Coop to bring forward the truth, but for now, it had to wait.

"I'm terribly sorry to hear that. I take it he's on the transplant list?"

"Yes, he is. Me, my mom, and some of his co-workers have been tested to see if any of us can donate a kidney. Hopefully one of us can do it. We should find out later today. As you know, Jackson helped me last year with Nathan, Jacob, and Brett, and he has since become like a big brother to me, so I want to do everything I can to help him out."

Principal Owen nods twice. "I take it you are here in my office for a reason. What can I do to help?"

Coop hands the notebook to Principal Owen. "After visiting Jackson in the hospital last night, a plan started to form in my head, so when I got home I wrote the whole thing down, but I need your help getting this thing off the ground. If you could just read through that real quick and let me know what you think, that would be awesome."

"Well, let's see what we have here."

"Thank you."

Principal Owen reads through the pages, careful as he turns from one page to the next, not wanting to accidently tear them out from the notebook. After finishing the final page, he turns back to the beginning and quickly reads through the pages again, just to clarify his thoughts. He stares at the first page for a while, deep in thought as he processes the information.

Coop's mind stirs with worry about his principal rejecting the ideas. So much of the plan hinges on Principal Owen accepting the course of action and playing a major role in getting it done. Doubt creeps into his mind about every little thing that could go wrong. *There is too much to do. There is so little time to accomplish everything. The logistics will be a nightmare. No one really cares. Principal Owen doesn't care enough to take part. Jackson won't find a match for a kidney. I will fail him as a friend, a brother. Jackson is going to die and it will be all my fault. I didn't try hard enough. My plan is not good enough.*

Coop is shaken from his anxiety-ridden trance by the voice of Principal Owen.

"Coop, I have to tell you," Marcus says as he shakes his head.

A pit forms in Coop's stomach and the acids churn, fighting to work their way up. "Give it to me straight," he squeaks out.

"As I was saying, Coop, this is ... extraordinary."

Coop's shoulders relax but he is still on alert for that age-old psychological trick of giving people bad news with a softening early blow of affirmation.

"And you came up with all this last night?" Marcus asks, incredulous.

Coop nods and rubs the back of his head with his left hand, still on edge about being turned away.

"I'm truly stunned. This is a remarkable thing you did here. So thorough. I ab ... so ... lutely ... love it!"

Coop's expels a deep, full body sigh. "Thank you. I just want my friend to live. I don't know how feasible all this is but I want to try, and I'm willing to work every minute of every day to see it done. Is there any chance? Please be honest."

Marcus rubs the underside of his chin with the back of right hand. "In all honesty, it's going to be difficult. The timeframe in which you hope to accomplish this is problematic, the resources available are limited, and quite frankly, I just don't know if there are enough hours in the day to get it all done this week."

Some of the hope falls from Coop's face and Principal Owen picks up on it.

"But," Marcus continues, putting up his right index finger. "We're sure as hell going to try. I'm with you, Coop. All the way."

Coop smiles wide. "Thank you so much!"

"Don't thank me yet. We have a lot of work to do if we're going to pull this off. I think we have an extraordinary opportunity here to enrich the students of this school, and maybe the community at large. Your story, your friendship with Jackson, all of it, needs to be shared and encouraged and used as an example of what life is really about."

"That's great news. I hope we can do it."

"I tell you what, why don't you leave the notebook with me, and I'll spend the morning trying to put some pieces into place while you're in class, and we'll sit down at lunch to discuss it further. How's that sound?"

"Sounds perfect. I don't know if I'm going to be able to concentrate in class today. My mind is reeling."

"Just do the best you can, and know I'm on top of this, you can trust in that."

"Okay."

Principal Owen stands. "You better get going. First period is starting soon. Just come back here at lunch and we'll talk more."

Coop nods and rises from his chair, zips his bag closed, and steps around the chair to leave. He reaches the door and stops momentarily to thank Principal Owen again, then he exits the office and hustles off to class.

CHAPTER TWENTY-TWO

Coop sits through first period English, barely paying attention to the lessons being taught. He stares off into the distance just thinking about his friend, near death in that sterile and gray hospital room, tubes and wires running everywhere. The beep of the monitors grating at his mind like a bell ringing right next to his ear. Every few seconds, his eyes dart to the clock above Mrs. Johnson's desk, and each time he questions whether the damn thing is broken. The arms appear to be going nowhere.

Second period Pre-Algebra is no better except he takes a quiz that occupies half the class time. Before class started, Mr. Thompson asked Coop how he was doing, as he could see the contemplative look in the boy's eyes, and Coop offered up a brief summary of the events that had taken place. Mr. Thompson understood his plight and allowed Coop to pretty much zone out after the quiz, realizing his best student had bigger things to think about than solving for x, y, and z.

In his final class before lunch, Social Studies, Coop manages to focus more, his mind finally settling down. Perhaps, after nearly thirty-six hours of nonstop Saving Jackson mode, his brain just makes the involuntary decision to rein it in for a time. For the first time since classes started that day, he does not look at the clock and is genuinely surprised to hear the bell ring at 11:05. He springs from his desk, packing up as he jogs off toward the principal's office.

Coop knocks on the frosted glass door.

"Come," shouts Principal Owen from his desk chair.

Coop enters and takes the same seat he had earlier in the day. He pulls a whole-grain strawberry cereal bar from the front pouch of his bag, tears it open, and begins munching on it.

Principal Owen grabs one of the two bottles of water from the edge of his desk and places one in front of Coop.

"I picked you up a water, if you want it."

"Thanks." Coop devours the rest of his cereal bar then takes two sips of water.

"Well, Coop, I've made some arrangements and it looks like we're going to be able to pull this whole thing together."

"Great. Thank you so much." He takes a few more small sips of water. "So, do tell. How is this going to happen?"

"Tomorrow during final period, we'll have an all-school assembly where I will talk about bullying and then I'll introduce you. You will come up and give a little speech about your and Jackson's relationship and anything else you care to share about bullying or whatever you need to. After that, you'll share the fundraising efforts I've arranged. Just focus on your friend, give a little background on your relationship. It's an important message and we could all use a little coaching on the subject."

"That sounds perfect."

"Just try to get your speech written at home tonight and I'll excuse you from fifth and sixth period tomorrow so we can go over it. How's that sound?"

Coop nods with excitement then takes a couple more sips of his water. "And what about the fundraising? Is there time enough to do some of that stuff?"

"It won't be easy, but yes. At the end of the assembly, we'll announce our plans to raise money. Bake sale, raffle ticket drawing, and we'll do one of those donor website things, create a Facebook page for Jackson, like you had suggested in your manifesto. If we hold the fundraising part here Thursday and Friday, I assume it can continue over the weekend on its own. That will give people Wednesday night and Thursday to get the baked goods together, and for us to get a few donated items to raffle off."

"Wow! That sounds perfect."

"Coop, I just want to say, I'm really proud of you. I'm impressed at how you've taken such a difficult situation and are working so hard to turn it into a positive one. Kudos to you."

"I think Jackson would do the same for me. If there is anything I can do to help save his life, then

I'm going to do it, period. That's what family is for, right?"

"I've never heard a better definition. You need anything more for lunch than that fruit bar?" Principal Owen doesn't wait for an answer. "Let's go down to the cafeteria and I'll buy you something more substantial. You're going to need the brain food."

Coop shrugs his shoulders but after thinking about it for a second, he realizes the principal is right. "Okay. Thank you."

Coop rises from his seat, chugs the rest of his water, and tosses the bottle in the recycle bin near Principal Owen's desk, the cereal bar wrapper into the trash bin.

Principal Owen stands up too, checks his front pockets to confirm his cell phone and keys are there, then they both leave the office together, heading toward the cafeteria.

The cafeteria is buzzing with clacking trays, squeaking chairs, and the chatter of children. The room is square with dozens of long white tables, each with eight chairs. The back wall is nothing but windows that allow the afternoon sunshine a place to enter. To the right, the serving line is dwindling from the first round of students.

Principal Owen and Coop join the food procession, each getting an identical tray of food consisting of breaded chicken nuggets, mashed potatoes, peas and carrots, an applesauce cup, and a 2% milk carton. Principal Owen pays for both.

They choose the table nearest the entrance, a table no one ever sits at unless there is no other place to use. They want the privacy for their chat, which seems obvious to the rest of the student body, as many students immediately start gossiping and pointing fingers in their direction. They pay no mind and eat their food without talking until Coop breaks the silence with some news he feels it is time to share, even though he's hesitant to do so.

"I should probably tell you about something that happened yesterday after school," Coop says, reluctance glued to every word.

"Oh? You mean, other than what happened to Jackson?"

Coop nods and points to his face. "You asked earlier about my face. Well, I had a little," Coop pauses to select his words carefully, "incident outside Jackson's apartment. I went over to his place, like I usually do on Mondays, but he wasn't home. Obviously, he was already in the hospital but I didn't know that at the time. So, I decided to just sit on the steps and wait for my mom to get there, do some reading. As my luck would have it, I spotted Brett, Jacob, and Nathan walking across the street."

Principal Owen cut off Coop, his face stern. "If you're going to tell me what I think you're going to tell me, somebody is in deep, deep trouble." He places his right hand up in contrition. "But go ahead, sorry to interrupt."

"Yeah, you're not going to like it."

"I was afraid of that."

"They saw me sitting there by myself and came over. Nathan and Jacob started hassling me, Brett just kind of stood there. I could tell he didn't really want to be involved. Anyway, they said things. I asked them to just leave me alone. Nathan put his hands on me but I fought back and we ended up on the ground. That was it, really. A guy that lives in the apartment complex came out and helped me, made the three of them run away. Once I got the news about Jackson, I just didn't care anymore."

Principal Owen shakes his head and sighs, loudly, like he was trying to blow down a house of cards on the table. "Sounds to me like those boys just earned themselves a nice, long suspension. I'm not going to tolerate that behavior and I made it pretty clear to them that we'll have no more of that tomfoolery or there will be dire consequences. Apparently, the message was not received, or just flat-out ignored." Principal Owen rises from his seat. "Have you seen any of them around here today?"

"Yes, but we didn't make eye contact. Coop puts his hands up, palms toward the principal. "Now, before you do anything, I'd like to consider the whole suspension thing."

"How do you mean?"

"I don't know, I just don't think kicking them out of school is going to change anything. It might with Jacob and Brett, they're just the followers, but Nathan, he's the instigator. From what I've heard, his mom is not around and his dad is not a nice person. That's just what I've heard. Certainly, there is something more we can do for them, especially Nathan. Something that will help him deal with whatever is triggering his need to pick on me."

A puzzled look draws across Principal Owen's face but he says nothing.

"I would much rather see some effort to rehabilitate him than to punish him. There's some good in him, he just needs a healthy outlet for his anger."

"My god, Coop. How old are you again? I probably need to send you over to the college to teach a Psych class. Wow. But I hear what you're saying, and to some degree, I'm sure you're right. I'll deal with them and I will definitely take your thoughts into consideration."

Coop stands and picks up his tray. "Okay. As mad as I am about what they did, I honestly feel more sorry for them than angry."

"That's an incredible stance to take, and that is exactly why your story is so important to share with the entire school ... and with the community. The level of compassion you're demonstrating is impressive, an important lesson we need to pass along."

"Knowledge and empathy over fear and hate, that's what I'm choosing. It's as simple as that."

"Again, you continue to dazzle me, Coop. You're like a young Dalai Lama." Principal Owen smiles, grabs his tray, and motions for them to leave.

Coop returns the grin and follows his lead. "I think I'm more channeling Jackson than anything. When I say the words, I hear his voice speaking to me."

They place their trays in the dirty dishes pass-thru and exit the cafeteria, stopping just outside to finish their conversation.

"Sounds like a smart guy." He glances at his watch and realizes he has a meeting and Coop's next class is beginning soon. "Well, Coop, I have appointments and you have class. Come see me tomorrow when you get in, and do your best to concentrate in classes the rest of the day." He pats Coop on the shoulder. "Okay, then?"

"I will. Thank you, and thanks for lunch."

They part ways, Coop heading down the west hall to his Earth Science class with Mr. Taylor, Principal Owen in the opposite direction to the administration wing to make a phone call from his office, all the while thinking about how and when he would deal with his three little troublemakers.

CHAPTER TWENTY-THREE

The tepid spring air glides across Coop's outstretched arm. He opens and closes his hand, alternating between fighting the pressure against his palm and the air hitting his knuckles. His head tilts toward the window too, the air much cooler on his face at thirty-five miles per hour than when standing still, the breeze rustling his hair, as relaxing a moment as he's had in forty-eight hours. As soon as he had entered the car, he rolled down his window to take advantage of the sooner than expected warm temperatures.

Four minutes into the ride home, Kelly speaks first. "You haven't said anything. Am I to assume that means your meeting with the principal went well or went crappy?" Her eyes stay locked on the road, her own window open only two inches.

"I'm sorry. I'm just zoned out and enjoying this warm weather. This is the first moment of calm I've had today."

"Okay. Well, spill it boy, I've been waiting all day to hear what happened." Kelly thinks about how much easier it would be when Coop gets his own cell phone. Cost has always been the issue keeping her from allowing him to have one. She certainly has no doubt in his maturity level. What Coop doesn't know is that Kelly is planning on getting him one for his next birthday. He'll be turning thirteen, and in this day and age, a teenager without a cell phone is almost unheard of, she keeps telling herself.

As she ponders the events of the last forty-eight hours, regret sweeps over her. *Would having a cell phone have prevented Coop's latest tussle with Nathan and the others. Oh god. What kind of mother am I? I'm so, so sorry baby.* She does not share this revelation with her son, though she's confident she'll be haunted by it for some time.

Coop pulls his arm in and rolls his window halfway up. "Geez, mother. Relax. It went great. I laid out my ideas for him and he pretty much jumped right onboard. He talked to some of the faculty and arranged for an assembly for Wednesday, followed by some fundraising efforts beginning Thursday. Which reminds me. We'll need to bake some cookies and brownies and cupcakes, maybe some lemon bars that we can offer at the bake sale."

"We? When you say we, you mean *me*, right?"

"Looooove yooooooou," Coop rebounds with the biggest puppy dog eyes and pouty lip he can muster. Batting his eyelashes, he adds, "Pleeeeeeeease." He holds the face as long as he can before breaking into a huge shit-eating grin.

"Of course I will, ya doofus. And you need that rather large list of fine baked goods for Thursday?"

"Yes. The bake sale is going to be Thursday and Friday before classes and at lunch. I'll help as much as I can, but I still have homework to do. Aaaaaand, I have to write a speech tonight to give at the assembly. Is it going to be a problem?"

"I'll make it happen. And, speaking of things you need to do tonight. I got a call from the hospital today."

"What's the matter? What happened?" Coop turns part way to face his mom, his eyes marked with alarm.

"Nothing like that. There has been no change with Jackson. It's the testing for a donor match. The results came back." Kelly pauses for a millisecond, allowing Coop to interject.

"And..."

"Gimme a chance. There was one match. As good a match as it could be without that person actually being related to Jackson." She takes a deep breath knowing what the words will mean. "It's you, Cooper." She never called him Cooper unless things had just gotten serious. "You're the one."

"Well, it's settled then. When do I do this thing?"

"Easy, tiger. It's not that simple. You still need some further evaluation before you are officially approved. I set up an appointment and we're on our way there now. It's a basic physical, some blood work. If that goes well," Kelly bobs her head from side to side, "they'll schedule a surgery right away, probably next Monday or Tuesday, I'm assuming."

"Okay. Well, that gives me time to get through all this prep work and my speech and the fundraising." The logistics and health implications of donating his kidney float around his mind but he can't quite grab onto all of it. There are just too many other things to worry about right now.

"I'll be honest with ya. I'd be lying if I told you I wasn't nervous about all this. Any surgery has risk. I just don't know what I would do ... if something happened," Kelly says, her voice quivering toward the end. She loses her battle to fight back the tears. She takes her left hand off the wheel, wipes the moisture from her eyes, and rubs the side of her hand under her nose. Somehow, she manages to keep her composure and not burst into full on bawling.

"I know, mom. I know. Please don't cry. Everything will be fine. I just know it. I don't know how, but I just know."

His confidence actually helps her. She knows she has no choice but to find a way to believe everything will work out in the end. Coping is the best she can do, and she must remain strong, composed. Her motherly instincts do not allow for anything else, and she embraces it. There'll be a time and place for worry, she thinks, but now is a time for strength. She regains composure, for Coop's sake.

"How did I end up with such a brilliant son?"

"You're just lucky, I guess."

They chuckle together and enjoy their moment of fun, ending the car conversation on that high note. The last few minutes of the drive to the hospital are silent and contemplative for both.

Coop's physical goes off without a hitch, so they head to Jackson's room for a quick visit before heading out. They briskly walk the long glass and steel corridors of the walkway between the buildings to reach the I.C.U. With dinner yet to be had, a grocery store trip to make, homework to do, and a speech to write, they both feel the time crunch.

They stop at the nurse's station to get an update on Jackson's condition. The charge nurse, a heavyset woman in her early fifties with short wavy blonde hair and standing just short of six feet tall, greets them without a smile, too busy to bother with formalities.

"What can I do for you folks?" She doesn't make eye contact, instead choosing to stay fixed on her computer screen.

"Our friend Jackson Reed is in Room 345 and we just want to get an update on his condition, see if anything has changed since yesterday," Kelly says.

"Oh. Jackson. At the moment, he is stable. There's nothing new to report. The dialysis is holding him steady for now. Getting a kidney soon is going to be paramount."

"Speaking of, my son, Coop," Kelly says while directing a hand at Coop. "We're just coming from his physical and blood work. It appears he will be the donor." She looks to her son with glowing pride on her face, apprehension in her eyes.

The nurse perks up. "So, you're the brave guy. That's a pretty great thing you're doing. And don't you worry. We're gonna take good care of both of you."

"I'm not worried. I just want to save my friend and put this whole thing behind us. Can we go in and see him real quick?"

"And you will save him, you will. And definitely, go right in."

"Thanks," Kelly says.

They rush off to Jackson's room. The door is wide open. Seeing Jackson in the hospital bed, a shadow of his former self and twenty pounds lighter, shocks them as much as it did the first time.

"I don't think I can ever get used to seeing him this way."

"Me neither, mom, me neither." Coop steps right up to the bedside of his friend.

Kelly stands at the end of the bed just staring at Jackson with a heavy heart.

"Good news, Jackson. I'm a match and we're going to do this thing and get you the hell outta here. Just please hang on." Coop places his right hand on the upper part of Jackson's arm. "Just hang on for a little while longer and everything is going to be okay. Things are going to be busy for the next few days but I promise I'll come back this weekend. I've got something I would like to read to you. You've been avoiding it, I know, but I figure this way, I can kind of force it on you, even if it's only subliminally." Coop smiles. "I'll see you soon.

"You ready?" Coop asks. "Got a lot to do tonight."

"Yep. Let's get out of here."

They swing by a fast food restaurant near their house to get a few burgers for dinner - a rare treat to save time. Kelly is already planning the grocery list in her mind of the ingredients she will need for the multitude of baked goods she will prepare on Wednesday. As soon as Coop asked her to prepare food for the bake sale, she made up her mind to call off of work for Wednesday. Coop would need to return to the hospital for more tests that day as well, so it was a no-brainer.

She plans to leave Coop at home after dinner to work on his speech while she goes out and shops. With the ingredients already purchased, she can get more accomplished early the next day.

Coop clears the last bite of his triple cheeseburger from the wax wraping that's doubling as a plate, then dips his last two fries in the diminishing smear of ketchup and takes them down. Finally, he cleans off the kitchen table, ready to begin working on his speech while the fire is still burning.

Kelly was used to eating at a more deliberate pace and had already finished her grilled chicken sandwich and small order of fries. She pulls her two master recipe books from a kitchen drawer and places them on the counter with a pad of paper and pencil. She quickly makes a list of items to purchase after doing mental calculations of any deficits.

Coop enters the living room and walks to the couch where he had placed his book bag after getting home. He removes a spiral notebook with a red cover and two #2 pencils, freshly sharpened at school.

In the kitchen, Coop takes a seat again at the table, flips to the middle of the notebook, chooses a pencil and places the other near the center of the table, and writes the words *Saving Jackson*, in the large upper section of the page.

He hears the rattle of his mom's car keys but pays it no mind. He's looking forward to his mother leaving for a time. Without distractions, he's more confident he will write a better speech, and quicker. The silence will help him focus. He'll be delivering a strong message and story to the entire school, and he has no desire to muck it up. Poignant and direct - words he stores in the forefront of his mind as he works.

CHAPTER TWENTY-FOUR

NEW MESSAGE

To – "Scoobydont69", "2NE1-KPopper",
"1LonelyGurl"

From – "ChickenCoop02"

Subject – RejectGuy99 is in the hospital and is very sick

Hello All,

I just wanted to let you guys know that RejectGuy99 is in the hospital and is not doing very well. He has been in a comatose state and desperately needs a kidney transplant. I realize that we all don't know each other outside of the game, but I know that he considers you all friends and I just thought I should let you know of his situation.

I'm just going to throw it out there and you can do as you will with the information, but Jackson Reed is at St. Mary's Hospital in room 345 should you want to pay him a visit. Again, he's in a coma, so I guess he won't really know you're there, but he could sure use the support.

I've been tested and am a match to donate a kidney to him, so I will be doing that early next week. I've talked to the principal of my school and we are having an assembly tomorrow to bring awareness to Jackson's situation and to try and raise money for the surgeries. We're doing a bake sale at Harrison Middle School Thursday and Friday, and I'm going to create a Facebook page tonight called SAVING JACKSON and I'll link it to a PayPal account to accept donations. He has no insurance, so needless to say, this whole thing is going to be expensive. If you can help out, please do.

I will be up at the hospital most of the day on Saturday and some on Sunday, so if you want to stop by then, I'd love to meet you all in person. I'll check my messages on here a few times a day, so if you need anything, let me know. Thanks.

I hope to hear from you or see you soon.

Your friend,

ChickenCoop02 (Cooper Dansbury)

NEW MESSAGE

To – "ChickenCoop02", "2NE1-KPopper", "1LonelyGurl"

From – "Scoobydont69"

Subject – RE: RejectGuy99 is in the hospital and is very sick

Hello Cooper & Everyone,

I'm stunned. I had no idea he was even sick. What the heck happened? When?

Is there anything I can do, specifically, to help out? Of course I'll go see him in the hospital. Thank you for letting us know. This is terrible. Does he have any family up there with him? I'll swing by first thing after work tomorrow, but I'll come back on Saturday too. My head is spinning here.

And since the cat is out of the bag now, I'm Seth Michaels. I look forward to meeting you on

Saturday, Cooper. Or sooner. I hate that it's under such dire circumstances.

NEW MESSAGE

To - "ScoobyDont69", "2NE1-KPopper", "1LonelyGurl"

From – "ChickenCoop02"

Subject – RE: RE: RejectGuy99 is in the hospital and is very sick

Thanks for replying Seth. I'm with you. This has all been a big surprise and a huge whirlwind.

In answer to your questions: Jackson has Polycystic Kidney Disease. (I'll let you google that one) He was hospitalized Monday after collapsing at work. Other than visiting him and donating (if you can), there is really nothing anyone can do. He has no family, save for my mom and me, at least in a surrogate sense. I'm not sure if you guys know 100% about his past, but his parents died when he was young and he was raised in a rough foster home but was never fully adopted. He doesn't speak with them, AT ALL, and he has no real family anywhere.

Hope to you see you on Saturday Seth. It's possible I could be up there tomorrow after school, but probably not. Too much to do.

Coop

NEW MESSAGE

To - "ScoobyDont69", "ChickenCoop02", "1LonelyGurl",

From - "2NE1-KPopper"

Subject - RE: RE: RE: RejectGuy99 is in the hospital and is very sick

OH MY GOD! I can't believe this. He never said anything about being sick. I'll be there Saturday. I can come about 10 am. And since we're on a roll with the big reveal, I'm Jason. I'm surprised after all this time that we've never met.

I wish there was something I could do to help. I hope LG reads this soon. She's gonna want to know.

And Cooper, donating your kidney is a pretty frickin' amazing thing to do. You're good peoples. What are the odds you guys were a match? Crazy. See you guys soon.

Jason Park

NEW MESSAGE

To - "ScoobyDont69", "2NE1-KPopper", "1LonelyGurl"

From – "ChickenCoop02"

Subject – RE: RE: RE: RE: RejectGuy99 is in the hospital and is very sick

Thanks Jason. Jackson means a lot to me, and I just wouldn't feel right if I didn't do everything I could to help him. I guess we'll see you Saturday then. Can't wait to meet all of you. And you guys can call me Coop. If anything changes, I'll message you. I'll also try to put regular updates on the Facebook page too.

Coop

CHAPTER TWENTY-FIVE

Through the backstage doors of the Harrison Middle School auditorium on Wednesday afternoon, Coop hears the murmur of the crowd, students and faculty waiting in their seats for the all-school assembly to begin. Not only is it audible, he can feel it, like the beginnings of an earthquake on the verge of kicking the seismologist's needle. He's been running the speech through his head since he put it to paper, and though he isn't nervous about the speaking part, he is apprehensive about the acceptance of his message.

The first phase of his master plan is being executed perfectly. Principal Owen spoke privately with all faculty members about what Coop hoped to achieve, and they all embraced the idea, if for no other reason, to use this unique situation as a teaching moment for the students, just as Principal Owen had envisioned from the get-go.

The squeal of a microphone from inside the auditorium breaks Coop from his train of thought. He stays put, but listens intently for his queue. Unknown time passes for him, like he is floating through space and then is instantly brought back to Earth in a flash of light.

"...So now I'd like to welcome to the stage, Cooper Dansbury, 7th grader here at Harrison, to tell you a story..."

Coop hears nothing else once his name is announced. He takes one last deep breath, pulls open the red backdoor of the auditorium, and marches toward the stage.

Principal Owen sees Coop enter the stage area, so he steps back from the worn, chipped, and lackluster mahogany podium. He pulls the plywood stepstool from beneath it, and motions Coop to step up.

They shake hands and Principal Owen leaves the front left of the stage down a rounded mini staircase, finding his seat in the first row, right next to his special guests: Nathan, Jacob, and Brett. After his meetings with Coop earlier in the week, Principal Owen called his three miscreants to his office, plucking them right out of class, and they each knew exactly what they were being called in for.

Nathan had Jacob convinced there was nothing the school could do since the incident happened after the final bell and off the grounds. *Besides*, he told the other two boys, *I don't think that little punk is going to tattle again. He's really going to start looking like a big baby if he does. I mean Christ, nothing really happened anyways.*

Brett did not buy into Nathan's confident jargon; instead, he counted on getting in trouble. He had been sweating bullets since he had gotten home that day, worried almost sick that their comeuppance would arrive, one way or another. Deep down, he wants to end his friendship with Nathan and Jacob but is too scared to do so; however, this may be the final straw.

Once all three boys entered and took a seat in Principal Owen's office, they were scolded for their behavior, their continual disrespect of the principal's authority, and the very serious offense of assault on another student.

Nathan started to explain his stance but was promptly interrupted with a fist pound on the desk, and loud enough to hear in the outer office and the hallway - *I don't want to hear your bull crap, Nathan.*

None of the boys spoke again during the meeting. They sat listening to the punishment laid down by their principal. They would not be suspended, as Principal Owen initially desired, which he thought would have been a perfect example and tone to set for the rest of the student body on bullying, but after considering Coop's words, he realized the better example would be one of knowledge, wisdom, and compassion.

The first stage of their reprimand is that they will be seated in the front row, right next to the principal, while Coop speaks, so they can feel first-hand how their actions have affected Coop at a mental and emotional level.

The second will be a personal apology to Coop, in private, as the principal has no intentions of humiliating them, though he did think about the effectiveness of such a public embarrassment in getting them to behave.

The third part will involve meeting with a school district psychologist a few times a month until the end of the school year. Principal Owen hopes that getting to the bottom of why the boys feel the need to continually torture Coop will lead to a breakthrough that will follow them for the rest of their lives.

Finally, all three boys will spend every Monday and Wednesday until June helping the janitors clean the bathrooms after school. Degrading? Yes, but he hopes effective.

Coop ascends the stepstool, taking his place behind the podium, adjusting the microphone lower to suit his height. From his back pocket he plucks a few note cards, though he's not sure he will need them. The words he wrote have been swirling in his mind like a mini tornado from the second he put down the pen after writing them.

He tweaks the position of the microphone one last time, shifts his eyeglasses higher on the bridge of his nose, and begins.

"Good afternoon everyone. My name is Cooper Dansbury. Most of you probably know me as Coop.

"About six months ago, I met someone not long after I came to this school, someone who came to my aid when I was being attacked ... for being different, for being quiet, for a being a little weird, maybe. Honestly, I don't really know why it happened. You'd have to ask the boys who bullied me. They left me a little bruised, crinkled my book, bent my glasses up, but I survived.

"And, as Principal Owen discussed, we need to find better ways to express our anger, our feelings of insecurity, or lack of ... something.

"But today, for me, this assembly is about so much more than that. That person that helped me, my friend, my brother, at least in spirit, Jackson Reed ... is dying." He pauses, the words nearly gutting him. Coop reads the first note card again to get back on track.

"Somehow, someway, even at twenty-eight years old, he needs a kidney transplant or he may not survive another couple of weeks. He has something known as PKD or Polycystic Kidney Disease, and the short of that is his kidneys are failing. He is a good person, with a kind heart, and he needs help. He stepped in to help me when I was being harassed, despite his own fears and past history with bullying. His parents died when he was young and he was raised by a truly awful foster family that neglected and abused him, his foster brothers harassing and picking on him constantly. He witnessed in my situation, something of his own life, and he couldn't stand by and watch me go through something similar. We can all learn a lesson from his actions and the lesson is - don't stand by and watch while others are being hurt, while others are down. And now, HE is down and I must do everything I can to help him.

"So, last night, I did some testing to be a donor, and as luck would have it, we are a match. Despite my mom's fear and her continually asking me to think hard about doing it before committing, the upsides and downsides, etcetera , etcetera, but there is no decision for me to make. I'm doing it. I don't NEED to think about it. To me, there are no downsides to saving Jackson's life. There ARE downsides to him being dead, that's all I know. Besides, he once saved me, so now I am simply returning the favor because that's what family does. They step forward and stand in the line of fire when needed. He needs it, so I am stepping forward. There is nothing more that needs to be said about that."

Coop flips his first note card to the back of the stack and glances quickly at the second one.

Before beginning again, he peeks in on the audience of the modestly lit auditorium. Everyone sits quiet, attentive. To his left, Coop sees Principal Owen and the three antagonists of his story. He refuses to look away when he and Nathan lock eyes, butterflies fluttering in his belly, but he can't be the first to break eye contact in their little game of chicken or Nathan's dominance will remain, so Coop thinks.

The second before the long pause in Coop's speech is becoming awkward, Nathan plays his part by lowering his head. Coop wastes no time in continuing, hoping Nathan is exercising true remorse.

"Now, I don't fully understand the other implications at play, primarily the financial side of it, so I've put together a plan that I feel will assist in that area as well. If a fundraiser has ever been called for to help out a worthy person, this is it. We must act fast. Time is short. Jackson's life is on the line."

Coop flips to his last note card titled: Fundraising. He can't read whether the audience, to this point, is receptive to his message, so he digs deep for a last burst of self-confidence, hoping he hasn't botched his one big chance to get everyone on board.

"As I just mentioned, raising some money is going to be key, as currently, Jackson has no health insurance. In order to do this, I've suggested to Principal Owen we hold a fundraiser, multiple fundraisers, actually, over the course of the next week, to raise as much money as we can to help with the many hospital bills that are already mounting, and ... will only grow, especially when my surgery and then Jackson's takes place.

"Here are some of the initial ideas for raising some money."

Coop flips his final note card to the back and continues.

"The first thing is to do a bake sale this Thursday and Friday, here at school. My mom has been generous enough to bake a great many things today that we can use, but if there is anyone out there who can help out by donating something tomorrow and or Friday, that would be great. Anyone interested should talk to Principal Owen for the details.

"The second thing to help raise money is selling some t-shirts, coffee mugs, and other things, probably next week, as it will take some time to get those together.

"And to summarize the rest so we can wrap this up, I created a Facebook page called, Saving Jackson, with links to a PayPal account for accepting cash donations. Please tell everyone you know about it, your parents, family, friends, and help spread the message. Every dollar will help.

"With all that being said, I implore you all to help where you can. I will be having surgery, either Monday or Tuesday next week, as Jackson's condition is dire, and the doctors want to do this thing as soon as possible to give him the best chance. I will donate one of my kidneys and with all the luck and kismet in the world, Jackson will receive the kidney with no rejection, and all of this will end happily ever after.

"Thank you for listening, thank you for helping. Thank you, thank you, thank you."

Coop steps down from the stool and away from the podium fighting his deepest emotions and the urge to cry. His speech was firm, direct, but it stirred the emotions of the crowd nonetheless. With perfect execution, every single person, adult and child, in the auditorium is touched by the strife of their fellow classmate and student, Cooper Dansbury, and his best bud, Jackson Reed. Without knowing how, Coop has set the audience member's hearts and minds on fire with the beat of his own and the language of his intellect.

Principal Owen promptly stands and begins clapping, slow and steady as everyone joins in, reaching a crescendo in ten seconds that forces Coop's feet to remain still just off stage. Without warning, Coop bursts into tears, letting his note cards fall to the floor before placing his hands over his face. All the stacked up, compartmentalized, and intangible emotion that he had not had time to deal with, to process, suddenly came bursting from his soul.

His body shakes and convulses with each wail from his heart. He shifts to his left and collapses into a gray aluminum folding chair sitting against the wall. The sobbing continues while the crowd clapping draws down.

Principal Owen hustles onto the stage and up to the podium.

"If anyone has questions about how they can help, please come see me or Mrs. Donovan. Please take a flyer from her on the way out. It has the Facebook page information on there. If anyone of you have parents that wouldn't mind prepping some baked goods for tomorrow or Friday, feel free to do it and bring them in. And please be courteous to the custodians and don't throw the flyers on the ground when you're done with them. Put them in a blue can. Thanks everybody. You're free to go."

The students and faculty rise from their seats and start exiting the auditorium, all of them ready to end the school day. Standing at the back, an unknown woman invited by Principal Owen finishes taking notes on a miniature yellow, legal notepad, packs away the pad and her pen in the oversized tote bag she carries on her shoulder, and then blends into the exiting crowd. Having a write-up in the local newspaper will help spread the word around town.

Principal Owen neglected to mention the reporter's invitation to Coop, not wanting to make him more nervous than he might have already been. She'll be waiting for them both in the hallway for a quick interview.

He turns from the podium and sees Coop sitting in on chair in the poorly lit back hallway just off stage. He walks over.

Coop is no longer crying, but sobbing softly and trying to gain his composure so he can leave. He alternates wiping the tears from his face and sniffing.

"Hey, Coop. That was incredible. You did a great job. How ya doing?"

"I'm okay. I got off stage and I just ... I just lost it." He runs his knuckles under his nose and stands. "It just kind of hit me all at once."

"Of course it did. That was a powerful speech you gave. Your best friend is in trouble and that's a scary situation. If I was in your shoes, I would've broken down long before now."

Coop knows it's not true but he appreciates the sentiment.

"Thanks."

Unsure whether Coop is a hugging kind of kid, Marcus goes for it anyway, wrapping his left arm around the boy's shoulders and drawing him somewhat near and patting him on the arm. "You did a good thing here today and it's going to help, big time. Trust me on that. But right now, I need you to get yourself together because we have someone waiting for us in the hall. Now, please forgive me for not saying anything to you about this, but I didn't want you to be nervous about the speech knowing that a reporter was going to be here to write an article about it." He releases Coop and faces him, reluctant to see his reaction.

Coop remains silent for a moment, furrowing his brow and biting his lip while processing the information and what it might mean for the cause.

"Awesome. Thank you. Why didn't I think of that?"

"Well, you sure as heck thought of everything else. She'd like to interview us right now. You okay with that? Putting this out to the general public sure could be a boost for the fundraising effort."

"Yes. My eyes are probably red." Coop takes in and releases a few deep breaths to calm down. "I think I can do it though."

"No pictures. She'll just ask a few questions and then we'll be on our way. Ready?"

"Ready."

CHAPTER TWENTY-SIX

Article in the Thursday morning edition of the local newspaper:

Local boy to donate kidney to best friend

by Victoria Yeltz

The city is abuzz with the heartfelt story of Jackson Reed, a PC hardware and software specialist at ACME Computer Repair and

Networking. He lays comatose and near death at St. Mary's Hospital in desperate need of a kidney transplant because of rare condition known as PKD or Polycystic Kidney Disease, whereby small tumors form on the kidneys over time, eventually inhibiting their ability to function properly. His best friend, Cooper Dansbury, a twelve-year-old Harrison Middle School student, has orchestrated a remarkable fundraising plan for his friend, and will now endure a major surgery and put his own life at risk to donate a kidney to save Jackson's life.

"Jackson is like a brother to me, and I just want to do everything I can to help him. It turns out we are match for kidney donation, so it's really a no-brainer for me," Cooper said.

As Coop described, earlier in the school year, they met when Jackson intervened after witnessing some boys picking on Coop near a baseball field. This event sparked a friendship that has grown and evolved into something extraordinary.

"Cooper has a unique mind and determination that is rarely seen in someone his age," Principal Marcus Owen said of his student. "When he heard the news that his friend Jackson was in the hospital and on the verge of death, he sat down that night and wrote up a three phase plan to save him. It's a remarkable story of friendship, tragedy, and selflessness. Throw on top of that the underlying story behind how they came to be friends, the bullying, the mentorship - you really have the making of something great here."

When Cooper presented the fundraising idea to him, Principal Owen took immediate action, scheduling an all-school assembly to discuss bullying and how the faculty and students could combat it, as well as to give Cooper a forum to share his and Jackson's story. The school is holding a bake sale today and Friday to raise money for the surgeries and aftercare.

If you would like to make a donation, please visit the Westside Bank and Trust and mention Jackson Reed or Cooper Dansbury, or go to: www.facebook.com/savingjackson to donate via PayPal and to show your support. ACME Computer Repair and Networking on South Washington is also accepting donations if you happen to stop in.

***

All the local television news outlets carry the story, bringing further attention to Coop's campaign. In businesses and households all over the city, people react:

"You hear about that kid who's donating a kidney to that guy in a coma at St. Mary's?" a man asks his wife as he reads the Friday morning paper.

"Karen was talking about it at work. That kid is doing a good thing. Should we give a little something?"

The man shrugs his shoulders. "Sure. We could spare twenty bucks. Just PayPal it."

"Great," the woman says.

Friday afternoon, around 2 p.m. at ACME, Meghan stands at the counter jotting down a list of things she needs to accomplish by the end of the day. Carlos and Henry are in the workshop trying to finish up the day's load of repairs and installs, struggling to keep up in Jackson's absence.

The bell rings as the entrance door opens. A man unfamiliar to Meghan walks in wearing a highly appointed suit and tie, and shoes Meghan is sure cost more than what she makes in a week at ACME. She thinks to herself - *doesn't this guy have PEOPLE that run his errands. What the heck is he doing down here?*

"Hi. What can I do for you?" Meghan asks with a sincere and big smile and no evidence of the crazy thoughts she has running through her head.

"Hello. I saw that story on the news this morning about Jackson Reed, the guy in the hospital needing a kidney transplant. Is this the place where he works?"

"Yes, it sure is. Terrible isn't it? We've all been worried sick around here."

"I bet you have. That was a nice piece they did on him this morning on the news, about how he helped that kid when he was getting bullied. Now he's donating a kidney to save him. Extraordinary."

"He's a brave one, that Coop. Who knows what would happen if he wasn't doing this."

"Indeed. Well, I was touched by the story, having endured some bullying when I was a kid, so I just wanted to give a little something to help out the cause."

"Oh, yeah." Meghan reaches down to the end of the counter and slides the one-gallon glass jar between them. Its metal lid had a three-inch wide slot cut into it. The jar itself has two inches of coin on the bottom and is half full of indiscernible bills.

"Perfect." The businessman pulls a prewritten and folded check from his inside suit coat pocket. "I made it out to cash, so be careful with it." He places the check through the slot. "I hope everything works out okay for Jackson and Cooper."

"We've been praying nonstop. Thanks for the support. It means a lot. By the way, I feel like I've seen you somewhere before. Do we know each another?"

"Are you flirting with me?" he jokes, but she doesn't know that.

"No, no. That's not what I meant at all." Her face turns bright red and she places her hand over her mouth.

"I'm just messing with you. I have one of those faces."

From the doorway leading to the break room, Henry peeks into the front of the store to see who had entered. His eyes light up at the sight of the businessman.

Meghan takes her hand away from her mouth. "Oh. Maybe that's it."

"Well, I do need to run. Good luck. I'll be following the story. I'm confident things will turn out well in the end. Have a nice day." The man waves and doesn't wait for a response. Before Meghan knows it, he has exited the building.

Henry emerges from the doorway. "Hey. Wow. What the heck did he want?"

"He made a donation to Jackson. Why do say *wow*?"

"Why? Don't you know who that was?"

"No, though he did look familiar. Who was it?"

"Aaron ... Hartley. Owner of Hartley Enterprises. Might be the richest guy in this town."

"Oh ... my ... god. I thought I recognized him. Doesn't he own like three restaurants?

"Among other things. He was a major player in that new mall on the north side of town."

It dawns on Meghan that this man they are speaking of just dropped a check in their donation jar. She cannot contain her curiosity. She palms the aluminum lid with her right hand, securing the jar with her left, then twists three times.

"What are you doing?" Henry asks.

She ignores his words and removes the check from the jar, opening it to reveal the dirty, little details of the rich man's endowment. Meghan's face displays sheer awe.

"Well, how much is it?" Henry doesn't wait for an answer. "How much?" he begs.

Meghan swallows hard and tries to speak but she can't say the words past an F sound. Instead, she holds up the check with both hands and flips it around to show Henry.

"Holy shit!" He slaps his hand over his mouth, embarrassed by his crass language. "I'm sorry. That was inappropriate."

Meghan stands in shock at Henry's cussing, even knowing the dollar amount on the check. He never cusses in front of her, and he almost never does outside of work either.

"Fifty thousand dollars! Holy mackerel!" Henry realizes he's breathing heavy, so he makes a conscientious effort to calm down by drawing in a deep breath, through his nose and out of his mouth. "Wow. That is incredibly generous."

"Hang on." Meghan puts up a finger and races past Henry to the back room.

She didn't see him immediately so she yells, "Carlos!"

He pops up from a crouching position near the back corner of the workshop. "Yeah. What's up?"

"This super rich guy just dropped over a check for fifty thousand dollars for Jackson. Can you believe that? We about crapped."

"Fifty thousand? No way. That is sweet."

"Yeah it is. What a nice guy, huh?"

Carlos nods and crouches back down to continue searching for a hard drive.

Meghan starts to return to the front but stops at the break room when she sees that Henry has moved there and is sitting at the long banquet table. He is visibly upset.

"Are you okay? What's the matter?" Meghan asks.

He looks to her with dread in his eyes. "He's gonna be okay, right? I mean, they're both gonna be okay?"

She walks over to Henry and puts her arm around him. "Of course they're going to be okay. They just have to be."

RICHARD A. POWELL II

CHAPTER TWENTY-SEVEN

After the busiest and most stressful week of young Coop's life, he settles into a bedside chair next to Jackson on Saturday mid-morning. His mother needed to run some errands and clean the house, so she dropped Coop off around 9 a.m. so he could spend time with his friend, unwind a little from the tumultuous week, and hopefully meet a few gamer friends.

Coop continues to hold onto to the idea that Jackson is somehow conscious of his surroundings, regardless of the coma, and since the time had come for them both to begin their next shared book, he decides to begin reading the selection aloud to Jackson.

"Well, you said it was about time for both of us to man-up a little, so I figured we go ahead and bump Fight Club to the top of the list for our reading club. Plus, it fairly short, so it won't be a problem getting through it this weekend, as long as they don't throw me outta here."

Coop checks the clock on the wall opposite the bed and sees it is 9:30. He looks back to Jackson. "And, I hope you don't kill me later, but some of our gamer buds might come and visit. I know you won't be *meeting* meeting them, but you should feel good that you have people in your life that care enough to come down here to see you, even if they have been, up until now, only virtual friends. And have no fear. Your foster family has not been made aware of your situation, unless they heard about it on the news, so no visit from them. From the second we got here, I insisted they not be told or you would be pissed. You can thank me later for that one."

Coop reads for thirty minutes in their book club selection. He stops a few times and asks Jackson a question about a particular passage or if he has ever had insomnia. He has no desire to stop reading but does so when two strangers tentatively enter the room.

The taller, older man steps forward. "Hi there. Coop?"

Coop uses a slip of paper from the bedside table as a bookmark, then stands up, placing the book on the seat of the chair.

"Yep. Hi. What can I do for you?"

"You're almost exactly like I imagined you. Sorry. I'm Seth." He throws up a mini-wave then stands aside to let the other man forward.

"Hi, Coop. Jason Park, otherwise known as KPOP." At about five and a half feet tall, he's barely taller than Coop who had sprouted to five feet, four inches tall after being five foot at the start of the school year. Seth towers over both of them at six feet, two inches tall, his graying around the temples typical of a man in his early forties.

"Oh my god. I'm so glad you guys came. Come on in." Coop steps to the end of the bed to make way for his friends to go bedside. He waves them in. "Well, this is Jackson, otherwise known as RejectGuy99."

Seth and Jason come forward, Seth taking the lead while Jason stays closer to the end of the bed.

"He really isn't looking like his usual self," Coop defends. "He's lost some weight since being here and the tubes and wires aren't really doing much for his appearance either."

"I really hate seeing him for the first time in such a state. I sure hope he's going to be okay." Seth studies Jackson's face with regrets about not meeting sooner. "What's the prognosis?"

"Monday morning, they're removing one of my kidneys and giving it to him. Hopefully, it will take and everything will be fine. Back to normal in a few months. I assume you guys have heard the whole story on the news? And has anyone heard from LG?"

"I read it in the paper. Pretty amazing stuff. And no, I haven't heard from her, but I haven't checked since last night. Jason?"

"Nope. I logged in this morning and nothing."

"That's really weird," Seth says. "She's usually diligent about checking her messages. I hope everything is okay."

"I'm sure she just got busy," Jason adds.

Coop nods. "I just hope she checks in soon. Heaven forbid. If something bad were to happen, she might be pretty upset about not being able to be here. I mean, it's not just me? She and Jackson kind of have a thing, right?" At least as much as you can have *a thing* online."

"Of course they do," Seth answers.

Jason nods vigorously with a smirk. "They've been batting that ball around since almost the very beginning. But you guys know RG ... I mean Jackson. For whatever reason, he's always avoided the big meet-up."

"Having gotten to know him pretty well, I can say the biggest problem is self-esteem. He wants it, but he doesn't feel like he deserves it." Coop shuffles his feet and LG comes to mind. "And, if he were to fall for someone, he just doesn't see how that woman could love him back. He's told me that almost word for word."

"There's someone for everybody, maybe even a few," Seth says with a grin.

Jason and Coop join Seth in a laugh.

"You interested in girls yet, Coop? You're twelve, thirteen, right?" Jason asks.

"Thirteen this year, and yeah I like girls, I just ... I don't know. I guess there's *one*."

"Oooooo. She cute?" Jason inquires.

"I ... well," Coop stammers.

"Don't bother the kid, Jason. You're embarrassing him."

"He knows I'm just messing with him. Plenty of time for girls. Right, Coop?"

Coop agrees.

"Well, I don't know about you guys, but I plan on sticking around for a little while. What do you say at eleven o'clock, we go down to the cafeteria and I'll buy us all lunch?" Seth suggests.

"Sounds good to me. I ain't got nowhere to be." Jason says.

"I plan on being here most of the day, so definitely. Thanks, Seth. That's very nice of you."

"My pleasure. So what have you been doing, watching TV or something?" Seth spots the book on the chair. "That's rather mature for someone your age, but then again, you seem like an old soul."

"I'm reading it to Jackson. We have a book club thing. We both read the same book once a month so we can discuss it. I read way more than he does, but ever since he met me, he's tried to read more. He used to a lot when he was younger."

"Younger than what? He's not even thirty," Seth jokingly says.

"When he was in high school, I guess. Mostly plays video games now, but you guys know that. Duh."

"I don't think it would be a stretch to say we all could do a lot more reading and a lot less game playing," Seth says

"I do enough reading for class," Jason says. "There's no way I'm reading any more than that, at least not 'til I'm out of school. Playing games is the only thing I have to wind down with between all the studying."

"Fair enough," Seth responds.

Coop reaches up and stretches. Forty-five straight minutes in an uncomfortable bedside chair has made him stiff. "I really need to stretch my legs. You guys wanna go for a quick walk before we eat lunch?"

"Sure," Seth responds.

Jason nods.

"Great." Coop leads them out of the room.

They walk the corridors leading to the cafeteria, discussing everything from the particulars of how Coop and Jackson met, to the events of the week at school, as well as, some of the details of Jackson's past and disastrous foster family experiences.

The conversation continues through their meal, after which, Seth and Jason depart with well-wishing and promises to check in early in the week.

Upon returning to Jackson's room, Coop notices a fresh bouquet of flowers on the table near the window. He walks over to see who they are from. The card attached to the red plastic stick near the front of the vase says: "Good luck with the surgery. Keeping you in our prayers. Henry, Carlos, and Meghan."

"You just missed him," alerts the nurse as he enters the room.

Coop jumps a little and spins around. "Oh, you scared the crap out of me."

"Sorry." Nurse Jamie Keyser hustles around the room, checking connections and dials and measurements. "The guy who dropped those off just left ... uhhhh ... Carlos, I think his name is."

"Oh. Sorry I missed him. He works with Jackson at ACME. I was hoping to say hi to him. Oh well. That was nice of him to stop by."

"Yep." Jaime keeps busy, very much in a hurry to get his work done.

"Hey, do you know Nurse Jensen?"

"Sure do."

"Do you know when she works next?" Coop had grown fond of her, even in the few encounters he had with her before she seemingly disappeared from the I.C.U. He hopes she will be around Monday and Tuesday post surgeries.

"She'll be here on Monday."

"Oh good. I like her." Coop realizes he might have offended Jaime. "Not that there's anything wrong with," he stumbles over his words, "I didn't mean," Coop stammers.

"No worries kid. She's awesome and you'll be lucky to have her."

Coop nods and smiles.

"I'll be back in thirty minutes, if you're still going to be around. Have a good one."

"Thanks. I'll be here."

Jaime exits the room.

Coop returns to the bedside chair, picking up the book before sitting down.

"Seth and Jason came by for visit, in case you're not aware. They are super nice and you're really going to like them. Hopefully LG surfaces soon."

Coop flips open the book to where he left off and continues reading aloud.

CHAPTER TWENTY-EIGHT

"Well kiddo, the time has come to do the deed. You have nothing to worry about. This staff is top notch, and I'm not just saying that because I'm part of it." Nurse Jensen's smile puts Coop at ease, though he's not as worried as he should be.

Coop is far more concerned about his friend, whose life hangs in the balance. His donation may be Jackson's last and best hope. Any surgery, especially one involving the removal of an organ, has its peril, but in his mind, Coop has set aside the worry about his own life, instead choosing to focus all the positive energy he can muster for his dear friend.

"How's Jackson?"

"He's doing okay, but this couldn't be happening at a better time. He's hanging on but barely."

"I'm ready to do this then. He saved me once and I owe him more than he'll ever know."

"It really is incredible what you're doing. Not many people could do this. Your mom told me everything you did this past week, raising all that money and now donating a kidney. It's simply remarkable."

"He would do the same for me."

"You mentioned he saved you? If you don't mind me asking, how was it he did that?"

"Well, near the beginning of the school year, I was sitting by myself, just reading near the baseball field after school, and these three jerks came over and started messing with me, grabbed my book and tossed it, among other things. Jackson happened to be walking by, which was weird because he normally gets off the bus by his apartment. That day, he missed his stop and had to exit near my school."

Nurse Jensen is busy rearranging the tubes and cords next to Coop's bed in preparation for moving him to the surgical wing, but as the details of the story emerge, her ears perk up at the familiarity of the account. She stops and faces Coop directly.

Coop wonders why she is suddenly so alert but doesn't bother asking why. "Anyway, he saw me getting picked on and came over and stopped those guys. They got in big trouble after I told my mom about what happened and we talked to the principal about it."

Courtney's eyes are so wide and her mouth agape at this point, Coop has no choice but inquire.

"Nurse Jensen, are you okay?"

"Coop, honey, this sounds so familiar to me." She unexpectedly remembers where she had heard the story before. "No way!"

"What? Tell me."

"Does the name RejectGuy99 mean anything to you?"

"I knew it! The first time we met, you said something that caught my attention but it didn't dawn on me at the time. Be back later, off to save a life?" Coop playfully points at Nurse Jensen with his right index finger. "You're LG, 1LonelyGurl."

Coop smiles like he just discovered a gold mine under his bed.

Nurse Jensen throws her head back, closes her eyes, and just laughs.

"Am I right? That's you. And yes, RejectGuy99 is Jackson's gamer alias. And I'm ChickenCoop02." Coop slaps both his hands on top of his head in a combination of disbelief and elation at the discovery.

Nurse Jensen stops laughing and looks back to Coop. She wipes the joyful tears from her eyes. "Oh, Coop. Of course that's me. Of course, of course, of course. What are the chances?"

"LG, this is crazy."

"Oh, you can call me Courtney. Apparently, we've known each other longer than we realized. Ha!"

"Well, Courtney, speaking of real names, we were all wondering what happened to you. I had an email exchange with the gamer team after Jackson went into the hospital but you never answered. We were all worried something had happened to you. And, I got to meet KPop and Scoob on Saturday. They came up here to visit Jackson. Jason and Seth are their real names. They're super cool guys."

"Oh no, sorry. I still can't believe all this. And you got to meet the guys? That's awesome." Courtney takes in a few deep breathes trying to gain composure. She puts her right hand over her mouth, quickly removing it again to speak. She talks fast. "My computer went down and I've been too busy to even check my email this week." She pauses for a second to wipe more tears from her face then continues. "I'm in the middle of a double shifts and have been so busy since coming back from visiting my mom. Oh my god. This is crazy. This is so crazy."

"Yeah. Absolutely nutty is what it is. I don't know if I should say this or not, but considering the circumstances and how our reject guy here can be a little slow in taking care of his own happiness ... well, ya know he's in love with you, right?"

Courtney cocks her head to the side like she has no idea what the boy is talking about, but in truth, she already knows, and in this moment, her own feelings for Jackson emerge from deep inside her heart, revealing themselves as clearly to her as knowing her own name.

She inhales and exhales, each one deep and slow. "Truth is, we've danced around it ever since our first days of gaming together, but he always seemed to have a reason for not wanting to meet."

"His self-esteem is pitiful. He doesn't feel like he deserves to have anything good, though in recent months, he has started to come around. When we talk about you though, he gets all weird. And it was pretty evident when I started gaming with you guys that there was a little something going on between you two. You may have to make the first move or poof." Coop thrusts his fingers from his palms to demonstrate something disappearing. "Or it'll be gone."

"You're a little too smart for your own good there, Chicken Coop," she says with a smile. "But yes, you're probably right. And I'll tell you what, you guys get through these surgeries, get yourselves back to full health, and after that, I won't waste another minute holding back. Life is too damn short to wait around for things to happen. You gotta go get what you want, right?"

Coop grins and nods, incredibly happy to have discovered something so wonderful just before surgery.

Nurse Jensen glances at the clock. "Oh goodness. It's time. I'll be right back and then off we go. I have a great feeling about all this. So great." She heads out of the room to get assistance with transport.

Just outside the room, Kelly waits, rubbing her hands nervously. She needs to go in and talk to her son, comfort him, but she can't bring herself to do it. She can't bear the thought of seeing his face knowing it could be the last time. *People die every day during routine surgeries*, she keeps saying in her head. *I shouldn't let him do this, but if I don't and Jackson dies, he'll never forgive me. Oh god. Please just let them both come through okay. Please, please, please.*

She hovers on the edge of tears just thinking about the dangers.

As Nurse Jensen walks by, she sees the turmoil in Kelly's eyes and stops. The previous moment's revelations about Jackson had put a smile on her face, so she quickly switches to a more solemn one for talking to Kelly. "Don't worry. Everything is going to be fine." She pats Kelly's left, upper arm. "We're going to take good care of him. You should go talk to him. We're getting ready to take him in." She pauses and thinks about revealing who she is, but decides to hold off. She pats Kelly again, this time on the hand, then rushes off to notify transport they are ready to move Coop.

Kelly heeds the advice and goes back in the room, walking straight to the bedside of her son.

The smile on Coop's face makes her wonder what he's been up to.

"So, what were the two of you talking about?"

"Do you know who that is?"

"Who? Nurse Jensen? Yeah ... it's Nurse Jensen."

"Oh, mom. She's so much more than that. You know that online game Jackson showed me how to play?"

"Yes."

"She's one of our teammates. Can you believe that?"

Kelly's eyes tell the whole story of her incredulity. She gulps hard and tries to grapple with the news.

"Jackson and I have been playing the game with her all this time, and now she's our nurse and none of us knew it. How awesome is that?"

"Oh my god!" Kelly slaps the top of her head with her left hand. "It truly is a small world. Here you met Seth and Jason on Saturday, and now Courtney, aaaaaand ... she's your nurse. I'm stunned. I ... I don't know what to say. That's so weird."

"I know, right? And, I don't know if I should have done it, but I told her that Jackson was in love with her, but she seemed to kind of know already, and I think she feels the same way."

"Are you serious? But they've never even met in real life."

"Yeah, but they flirt all the time while we play. But you know Jackson, always too big a chicken to meet up with these people. Well, the cat's out of the bag on that one. He's got no choice now."

"I suppose not."

"I hope he's not too pissed about it when he wakes up."

"After he hears what you've done for him, pissed will be the last thing he could ever be. A little perturbed maybe." Kelly winks. "He'll get over it. She's cute and funny too. He'd be lucky to wrangle that cowgirl."

Coop offers up a vigorous series of nods.

"Well, Coop honey. There's no more avoiding it. They're gonna be here any second to take you off to surgery. How you feeling about it?"

"I feel great about it, a little nervous, but not for me. I just need this whole thing to work for Jackson." Coop sees his mother's eyes well up, so he grabs her hand and squeezes, and she squeezes right back.

"I love you, son."

"I love you too, mom."

A man and woman from the transport department enter the room. Kelly stands back to let them work.

III

CHAPTER TWENTY-NINE

I peel open my eyes, slow. I'm groggy and my whole body, eyelids included, feels heavy. I don't recognize where I am. I'm flummoxed and can't focus on anything no matter how hard I try. Something elusive begins to surface in my head. A diner. It's busy. I need to go in. I have something to ask her before it is too late.

I turn my head and there she is. I've waited for this moment for a while now, just have to man up.

"Lorraine, my density has popped me to you," I mumble.

"What," the woman answers as she turns to give her full attention.

"Oh, what I meant to say was ... I'm your density, I mean ... your destiny."

I can see her smile wide and hope that means she is charmed beyond measure.

"Oh, I love that movie too, but I think the anesthesia has a got you a little sorted, honey. You just rest for a while ... RejectGuy99." An even bigger smile draws across her face. "You've had a tough week but you're doing okay now," Nurse Jensen adds.

"The Enchantment Under the Sea Dance," I mutter.

Wait. What did she call me?

My mind fades. I close my eyes.

I'm awake again, though confusion spins me. The last thing I can remember is a scene from Back to the Future, but not much else.

The room I'm in is lit but dim, soft and fluorescent. I recognize the space as a hospital room. I just don't understand what I'm doing here.

RICHARD A. POWELL II

I'm on my side and when I try and shift to my back, shooting pain alerts me as to why, so I settle right back to the position I awoke to.

I'm getting little flashes now. An ambulance ride, excruciating pain, and again – George McFly? RejectGuy99. Weird.

A woman I vaguely recognize enters the room and comes straight to my bedside with a big smile on her face.

"I see you're awake again. Thinking any more clearly now?"

She wastes no time busying herself by checking the monitors that are attached to wires, wires that snake and twist and eventually end up attached to some part of me.

Her voice is sweet, sincere, and I detect a little Midwest-Southern. She's ... womanly, to put it delicately, but cute as hell and she walks and talks with confidence - things I lack. They do say opposites attract, so there's that.

"Ummm ... I don't know. Not really sure how I got here or why I'm here. Care to fill me in on the gory details?" I place my right hand on my back and give her a wince, more with my face than audibly. "My back is killing me."

The nurse presses a button on one of the machines in response to my statement about the pain.

"There, that should help. A little morphine will do the trick. By the way, I'm Nurse Jensen, but you can call me Courtney."

"Thank you ... Courtney. So?" I ask with anticipation.

"Well, Jackson, a week ago, you collapsed at work, went unconscious. Your boss, Henry, called for an ambulance and you were brought in."

That must be the ambulance ride I barely remember.

"A week ago? Wow. I take it you guys have figured out what's wrong with me?"

"We sure did. You have something called PKD, polycystic kidney disease. On top of that, you had untreated diabetes which aggravated your already damaged kidneys."

My eyes go wide.

Courtney continues, "Aaaaand ... one of your kidneys had scar tissue from a previous, much older injury, reducing the function even further. So, you were basically a ticking time bomb."

"Oh boy, that all sounds very serious. Polycystic kidney disease? What in the world is that and can it be fixed?"

"The short answer, PKD causes little non-cancerous cysts to form on your kidneys, and unfortunately, there is no cure. As for fixing you, well, yes we did, and if all goes to plan, you'll be fine. But you're not out of the woods yet. There is still a chance your new kidney will not take, though we're very hopeful. Your donor was as a close a match as one can get without being related. That combined with the best anti-rejection drugs we have, the prognosis is excellent."

"Are you saying ... I received a kidney transplant? Holy shitballs." In my nervous state over the news I'm hearing, I try again to turn over and sit up. The pain is duller this time, allowing me to twist into an awkward half-leaning, half-laying position.

"You sure did, and just in time too. You were in a coma for a week and not doing well. That kidney came in just when things were getting dicey." Courtney comes over to me and straightens the tubes and wiring around me so they won't be pinched or snagged, then she adjusts my pillows to make my position more comfortable. "You almost died, Jackson."

"This ... this is crazy. I'd been having pain off and on for a while but I had no idea what the heck was wrong with me. Oh man, this is terrible. This has got to be expensive. I don't have the first idea how I'm going to pay for all this. I'll be ruined." I notice I'm breathing heavy, my heart racing, all the medical and fiscal details darting around in my head. What's the first thing I think of? There goes the car. Shit. Courtney notices my distress.

"You don't need to worry about that at the moment, so try to relax. Your only concern right now is in getting better. The rest can be dealt with later. Saving your life is priority number one. You got that mister?"

I nod and try to calm down. "Yes ma'am. This is just a lot to take in. I had no idea."

"Of course you didn't, silly. You were in a coma." We both smile.

I appreciate her efforts to ease my worry, but I can't keep my mind from racing. "So, can I ask? Who's the donor? Dead or alive?" I ask with a grimace, trying not to come off as morbid. I continue trying to control my breathing, glancing up at the heart monitor every few seconds to watch the number come down.

"Oh, he is very much alive," she says with a somewhat devious grin. Without moving her arm, she points to the other side of the room, behind me.

Pain be damned, I'm turning over. Slowly, with constant deep breaths and using my arms to brace my body, I shift, first to my back with a pit stop to analyze the sting, which is tolerable for now, and then I maneuver a quick shift-roll to finish.

I don't believe what I see. I'm baffled even. How can this be? My homeboy, my partner-in-crime, my adopted little nerd bro Coop is lying in a hospital bed on the other side of the room, soundly asleep, having just donated one of his kidneys to save me. Courtney just said I almost died, and Coop did that - for me?

I shut my eyes and put the back of my left hand over my mouth. I nearly cry, my lower lip quivering with an odd mix of anxiety, joy, love, and fear. What if something happens to him because of this and he...

I can't even say the word. Just the thought of it creates a huge lump in my stomach. I wipe the building moisture from my eyes and try to relax. I'm overwhelmed with gratitude and the idea that there is someone in the world who thought enough of me to be so generous. The emotion is overpowering.

I fall onto my back. "Is he ... okay?" I grimace from the pain.

"He's gonna be just fine. He came through the surgery perfectly, as did you. You're not one hundred percent out of the woods just yet, but everything looks great so far."

Phew. I can't believe Kelly let him do this. Then again, when the kid gets his mind on something, I can imagine he would have been difficult to negotiate with.

"I really, really have to tell you something. It's been killing me and I just can't hold it back anymore."

"Oh? What? Is everything okay?"

"Oh sorry, it's nothing like that. Your friend Coop over there told me the story about how the two of you met on the baseball field, and how you scared away those creeps, and the story sounded so familiar to me."

Embarrassment is written all over Jackson's face. "I can't believe he told you about that. And familiar how?"

"Well, I play this M-M-O-R-P-G and I remember one of my teammates telling a similar story. Craziest thing." She smiles slyly.

Even through the slight fog of meds, the pieces of this puzzle Courtney is describing itches at my brain. Out of nowhere, I remember something from earlier in the day - RejectGuy99. Someone called me that. I sit up from the pillows, bracing myself with hands flat to the mattress. At a million miles an hour, other words buzz around. Nurse Jensen. LG. BBL-OTSAL. Nurse Jensen. 1LonelyGurl. She's a nurse. There's no way. No ... fucking ... way!

I'm hyperventilating. Courtney gently pushes my shoulder to get me to lie back down.

"Try to relax. Take a deep breath."

I take one.

"Now let it out, nice and slow."

I do.

"Now take in another one, and let it out again, slowly."

She adjusts the oxygen tube under my nose to make it more comfortable but it's no use. These tubes are awkward and there's no making it better.

My heart rate is still pumping hard but my breathing is calmer.

"Are you?" I take in another long breath. "Are you ... LG?"

She closes her eyes for a second and takes her own advice about deep and rhythmic breathing. She can't help but smile and start to laugh.

"Oh, Jackson," Courtney says with pouty lips and watery eyes. "Yes. Yes. And you're RejectGuy99."

Instantly, I toil with what this development means. "Well, this is kind of a weird situation to meet under. I have to admit, I'm a little embarrassed. You've seen me all ... sickly, and..." My train of thought switches to an image of lying vulnerably in my hospital bed, no blankets, the only thing covering my body, a flimsy and see-through white gown, and Nurse Jensen-Courtney-LG, whatever I should call her, standing over me with a giant yellow sponge in hand. My eyes bulge with sheer horror.

"Oh, don't worry about it. You ain't got nuttin' I haven't seen a million times before, honey. But it's not like *I* bathed you or anything."

Oh crap. She's in my head now.

"The noobs and nursing assistants do most of the bathing around here."

So they did bath me, and that means *some* woman saw everything. Oh god! I think I'm going to hurl.

She senses my distress. "Jackson, Jackson, Jackson, we have so much to talk about now that the cat has jumped out of the bag. And we will, but right now, let's just leave all that behind and focus on getting you better. What do ya say?"

I nod and try to flush the negative thoughts from my head. Honestly, I'm having a hard time getting past the bathing situation. Ugh.

Immediate and cascading exhaustion takes hold of my being.

"I think I need to rest for a while." My eyes flutter.

"That's good," Courtney responds. "Maybe when you wake up we can get you some ice water."

"Okay." I think Courtney says something but I'm already zoning out. My eyes get heavier than I can hold.

CHAPTER THIRTY

I'm home now from my three week stay in the hospital. I was able to leave twelve days after the surgery, Coop after just a week. Oh, to have the healing power of a preteen. There were no complications for either of us, and lucky for Coop, he is smart enough to keep up with his classwork, despite using only textbooks and notes from his teachers. He will not need to go to summer school to make up any classes.

He and I had a long, deep conversation about what he did for me, but we waited until after we got out of the hospital to do it, privacy and all that. When our eyes met from our hospital beds for the first time, we both smiled, I waved and he waved back, and I said thank you and he said anytime. That was all that needed to be said in that moment for us both. A time would come later for us to get all weepy and hug it out and share our feelings, just not then. And that time came, and it was cathartic and soul-wrenching. I knew right then a bond had been formed that could never be broken. We are blood brothers now, or more accurately, organ brothers. Semantics.

Kelly has been stopping by to check on me daily, and I sincerely appreciate that. I allowed Henry to come by as well, his wife made me a lasagna, so let's be real, there was no saying no to that visit. Henry assured me my job was secure and just as soon as I was ready to get back to the grind, my position was waiting for me, and that everyone missed having me around. He also informed me that they hired two temp employees to cover some of my work, seeing as how Carlos was getting overwhelmed and business was growing. I told him I was anxious to get my life back to normal and that I would return the second

I felt up to doing it. A big part of putting this whole experience behind me will be getting back to ACME.

And speaking of work, I won't be back for at least another month. The doctors want to minimize my stress levels and limit my exposure to germs. I'm still taking immunosuppressive meds and will for some time. So far, there are no signs of rejection, which has led my gamer friends to start calling me No-RejectGuy99. Hardy har har.

I have my daily routines to ensure a safe and healthy recovery. They gave me a medical I.D. bracelet that I'm required to wear, in case of emergencies. My meds give me acne, a small price to pay for the gift of life, but it won't last forever. I've also been told to do regular self-breast and testicle exams to check for changes. Apparently, some of the meds can increase a person's chance of getting cancer. I hope to dodge that bomb.

I walk briefly every morning to keep my strength up, each time taking twenty more steps than the day before. Whenever I go outside, I'm required to be covered from head to toe to protect from the sun, so I wear pants and a hoodie, with the hoodie up as I walk down the street. In another week, I'll take enough steps to reach the convenient store. The sheer thought of being able to buy a few of my own groceries, even at exorbitant prices, will be worth its psychological weight in gold.

On a rather hilarious note, the hospital told me I may experience some dysfunction, sexually. HA! Is it possible to have dysfunction where function wasn't even happening? Oh, that's a riot. I admitted nothing, just nodded my head as the words came out of the nurse's mouth, and then acquiescing to take the advice, should the need arise. Pun NOT intended.

After waking from surgery, I insisted on having no visitors. I dreaded the idea of my fosters showing up. Not that they give a rat's ass, but regardless, I still didn't want to risk dealing with them. I needed no sympathy from those ass-clowns and just seeing their faces would have stressed me out so bad I probably would have busted a stitch and bled out. I took a pass on that garbage. More trash left out at the curb to help keep my mental garage clear.

I did send out a nice email to all my pals and co-workers who visited before the transplant, thanking them for their support and inviting them to a soon-to-be cookout once I feel better - a nice little summer kick-off celebration. It will be a perfect opportunity for me to thank everyone in person, and work toward expanding my personal friend bubble. I have always felt alone and hopeless and unconnected, but I know now that I was never really alone. I was just too scared to let people in, people who were right there under my chin.

Of course, I sure have a greater sense of community now. The fundraising campaign organized by Coop yielded slightly more than one hundred thousand dollars, about half of which came from a single donor: a rich, local businessman. The details of that were humbling and awe-inspiring. The hospital, a not-for-profit organization, also offered to pick up a significant part of the tab after hearing about my plight, Coop's incredible efforts, and our back story. A hospital representative came down to my room the day before I was discharged and told me the news. Sure took a load off my mind, more for the Dansburys than for myself. It would be one thing for me to have to deal with the economic consequences of all this crap, but if Kelly and Coop were to have to suffer financially for even one minute, I would have been heartbroken. Thank goodness that is not going to happen.

Courtney and I did have a discussion before I was discharged, and we both agreed to take things slow, our mutual affections obvious, our serendipitous meeting the perfect icebreaker. She has insisted on stopping by the apartment once a week to check on me, which I have no choice in refusing, because believe me, the tone of her voice made it clear she was going to show up with or without consent and would break the door in, if necessary. She got no lip from me on the matter.

Now, day after day, I embark on the journey of healing. I have good days and bad days, but overall, the process has been positive. I can't wait for my life to return to normal and for this whole affair to seem like a distant memory, maybe even so far away that it seems like it happened to someone else. I do realize, however, the scars will remind me and so will seeing Coop - my hero. Bravest kid ... hell, bravest human being I have ever known, and because of him, the world seems like a brighter and more inviting place, a place full of hope and possibilities and love. My enlightenment comes from that. When dark thoughts rise into view from sinister places, I can confidently stare back at them and say - I have looked death right in the face and yet I am alive.

What damage could you offer that would unravel *me*? None, that's what. None at all.

EPILOGUE

Well, it's been five years since the transplant, and the time has been a whirlwind, to say the least. If you had asked me a few years ago what lay ahead for me, I could not have answered with anything close to my current reality. I'm pretty much the luckiest sum-bitch alive. I do know that. So where do I begin?

I still participate in online gaming but only once a week. I have refused to change my screen name, RejectGuy99, so I have that constant reminder of my humble beginnings in the tech world, and of the man I used to be. I once believed I would never rise above my low station in life, never find happiness, never be anything but a reject. Lucky for me, the Universe stacked my team with all-stars, and when that late inning curveball came, I knocked it out of the park.

There is another gamer, however, that has changed her screen name as she just couldn't see fit to keep it. 1LonelyGurl is now NurseReed87. Oh ... did I mention Courtney and I are married now. Oh yeah, you read that right. And guess what? We have a three-year-old son - Leonard Cooper Reed. We call him LC.

Leonard is for Courtney's now passed grandfather on her mother's side, by all accounts, the kind of man that comes around only once a generation. He was generous by nature, always smiling and cracking jokes, shirt off his back kind of guy. I was delighted by the idea of paying tribute to him, even if by reputation alone.

Our son's middle name probably needs no explanation. His existence would not have been possible had my buddy, my brother, my best friend, Cooper Dansbury, not donated a piece of himself to save me, and orchestrate, quite frankly, the greatest short-term fundraising effort I have ever seen. To this day, I still cannot wrap my head around the whole affair. In one week's time, Coop went from finding out I was on death's door, to raising an obscene amount of money, to donating one of his kidneys, to saving my life. To say it out loud makes me feel quite inadequate. I'm absolutely certain I will never do anything so amazing. I would guess most of us won't.

Coop is about to graduate from high school, which is so crazy to me since I will always see him as that twelve-year-old kid laying in a hospital bed just across from my own, having just endured a surgery to donate a kidney to me and save my life. And he did, save my life, in more ways than one, and for that I can never truly repay him except maybe by continuing to steer him in the direction for greatness, which I guarantee he is bound for.

After giving his speech at the assembly on bullying, being in the news for his efforts to raise money for me, and donating a kidney, he made many new friends. His newfound celebrity brought a lot of attention from his classmates, mostly from girls, he reluctantly shared with me later. Eventually, he didn't mind so much all the notice from the fairer sex, but at the time, he took it in stride.

Once in high school, he became class president and was one B shy of a 4.00 grade point average. He had no trouble being accepted to multiple top universities. In the fall, he'll be attending the University of Illinois for Computer Engineering. There is no doubt in my mind he will dazzle. Of course, he's been working for me part-time over the summer at Reed Computer Repair & Networking, and he will be missed.

Reed Computer Repair & Networking? What about ACME? Well, ACME no longer exists. After much deliberation between Courtney and me after we got married, and a grand wedding gift from Courtney's parents, I bought ACME. I decided I wanted to be a bigger player in the software/hardware repair game, so I purchased a bigger facility, closed the old shop, and opened up the new one with a better business model and a different name. We now have twenty-eight employees and service the entire tri-county area. We even have company cars for all the local business travel, which is still a little weird to me considering I didn't even have my own car until a few short years ago. My, my how things have changed.

Carlos is still around and runs the back end as shop manager. He is my most trusted employee. I've rewarded his loyalty by giving him a 5 percent stake in the business. He has no ownership power per say, but I know it helps him to know that his position is more than just some geek job, it's a career and a real part of his life.

Henry stayed on as well and manages the front end. He has a 5 percent stake in the business too, which I felt was the least I could do for him. During my kidney fiasco, he was at the hospital every day and made sure I continued to get paid at full salary while I was down and out. He even let me work some from home during my healing process, allowing me to come back to the world of the living, gradually.

Meghan, the other employee from my final days at ACME, is now living in Florida and working as a Marketing Research Assistant with a major hospital conglomerate. She managed to finish her degree while working at ACME and has done well for herself, moving on to bigger and better things. She got married last year and now has a newborn baby girl named Sophie Hailee Martin. We sent along a nice baby arrival package from all of us at the company, and she returned to us a thank you card loaded with pictures of the happy family.

Of course, I haven't forgotten about Charlie, my old bus driver. He's still around and still driving bus Green #5. I jump on every once and a while for the Washington Street to Maple Avenue portion of his route, my old route, just to say hello and catch up. We're playfully formal with each other now. Hello, Mr. Reed, he says. Good afternoon, Mr. Halloway, I answer.

I recently asked him if he would come work for me in some capacity, maybe making deliveries.

He said, "I've been driving bus for so long, I don't think I know how to do anything else. And, I'm damn good at it."

"You ever think about retiring?" I asked.

"Retire?" he rebuked. "The key to happiness in life is to find something you love to do and do it with all your heart until the day you die ... or until they kick you out."

Hard to argue with that.

So what else can I say about my life, my loves, my work? The two sides of Jackson are now one big, happy, and healthy guy.

I'm just another business-owning, green-tea-drinking, always-getting-paid nerd, and now that I've filled my life with people I care about and that care about me, my awful past stays right where it belongs - in the rearview mirror of a car I don't drive anymore.

ABOUT THE AUTHOR

Richard A. Powell II currently lives with his wife Amy in Bloomington, Illinois, where he enjoys DIY projects, disc golf, technology, watching movies, playing video games, and reading and writing (obviously). He is also a self-professed nerd/geek, but no, he will not fix your computer, unless you ask really, really nicely and offer him a gift card to his favorite burger joint.